Chapel of Bones

A Novel

Joan Oltman

With love,
Joan Oltman

ISBN: 1539711404
ISBN 13: 9781539711407
Library of Congress Control Number: 2016918590
CreateSpace Independent Publishing Platform
North Charleston, South Carolina

Dedication

For Jim. How I wish you could see how this ended! I love you.

This book has so many godmothers, godfathers, guides, advisors, and editors, that they are beyond enumerating. If I leave any out, forgive me, you have been the fife and bugle corps that have kept me awake and marching. It has, however, only one culprit, me. I take full responsibility for all errors and infelicities.

To Patti Gauch, who said, "Everyone has a book in them."

To Sister Ruth Dowd, who wouldn't let me take just one class.

To Ruthe Feilbert-Willis, who's put up with a lot.

To Judy, Ivy, Ilene, and Janice, Martha's Godmothers, who must know it by heart and gave me their hearts all along the way.

To my daughters, Ellen and Cathy Megan, and son Jonathan, just because I love you.

To my grandchildren, Anna Rose, Rachel, Andrew, Noah, Rob, and Adam for the same reason.

To Aline Benjamin and so many people at Kendal who read it and gave me such good feedback.

To that nice couple who sat next to us at a sidewalk restaurant in Tarrytown, NY and asked to be notified when the book was published.

And to all the friends, neighbors, relatives, and acquaintances, who really didn't believe there would ever be a book,

THANK YOU

Preface

THIS BOOK IS purely a work of fiction and any resemblance to person or persons is coincidental. The story is made up. We never saw any ghosts, though not for lack of trying, and real places have been used combined with fictional places to create the sites described within.

How much is based on personal experience? Well, my husband and I, in the mid-twentieth century, studied for a year in England, while we were still undergraduates at Antioch College in Yellow Springs, Ohio. We were particularly intrigued by being in rooms and buildings and ruins that were hundreds, and in the case of Stonehenge, thousands, of years old. We would fantasize on what if we were the first people who had stood in this place, or touched this piece of stone, since the middle-ages or prehistoric times. That "what if" was the seed of this book. Lots of local people were happy to tell stories to two gullible yanks; and one showed us a small stone building behind a stout iron fence that had bones set into the mortar. He also took us to his local parish church, which had a leper's window and was reported to be where St. Augustine preached to the Kentish men, converting 10,000 of them on the spot.

Those two places became the setting for the story. The rest evolved from the many "what ifs" that developed over many years. And one thing led to another.

Table of Contents

1
Chapel of Bones 1952

TWO MEN, DRESSED in rough homespun tunics and carrying a stretcher between them, emerged through the heavy, closed door of the Chapel of Bones. As they trudged down the path, they gradually became transparent until they faded into nothingness.

I stared open-mouthed. Then I stumbled and Will grabbed my arm to keep me upright, as our guide, Mr. Cooper, turned and looked at me. It was obvious that Will had not seen them. "You ok?" he asked. I nodded, but my skin felt tight. All the sunny places seemed to shimmer in fluorescent colors.

The Chapel of Bones shimmered too. It looked very much like a photograph in the book I have carried everywhere with me since I was a girl. I could feel the worn volume poking my hip gently from within my backpack. The hexagonal little building was made of stone and mortar, with occasional courses of crumbling brick. The door was padlocked, and the windows, covered with grime, were almost slits with rounded tops. Right through the thick stone walls I could see the interior, the shelves lined with dead bodies, a large crucifix hanging on the wall opposite the door, a small stone altar. My heart was beating as though it would explode right out of my chest; I realized that this was it. This was truly why I had come to Canterbury!

What's more, despite the fact that this was the first time I had ever been in England, I felt absolutely certain that I had been in this place before.

Will and I had been married for less than six weeks. This trip to Canterbury was our first time out of London, where we had taken a bed-sitting flat and enrolled in classes at the University. All during the weeks since we marched down the gangplank in Southampton, we had been buying books, learning our way around the busses and the London underground, decorating the flat. But all the while, I had been restless, determined to get out of London.

Except for the book, into whose pages I could always enter, I hadn't experienced anything like the transparent men in several years. My life had filled with college and wonderful friends and new foods and Will. But in the few weeks since we had come to England, visions like this were appearing with greater frequency and far greater intensity. It seemed as though every time I slept, or went into a waking reverie, I would see medieval people: monks, knights, pages, farmers, all passing before my eyes, and over and over, I saw that tiny stone chapel. And each time I came close to a medieval building, my body tingled as though all the blood in my veins had evaporated. It was happening to me now.

We had walked into St. Martin's Lane on our hike from the youth hostel back into Canterbury. I had heard somewhere that there was a very old chapel to be seen here and I was searching for the structure shown in my book. I had become obsessed with finding it. I had this powerful feeling that if I could see it, enter it, I would understand why I had needed to get to England. I would begin to make sense to myself. Will trailed unenthusiastically behind me.

"Hey, Marti," Will called to me, his voice rising as though he had just thought of something wonderful, "there isn't anything here. Let's go look for the old St. Peter's in town." He was thumbing through the British Tourist Office's guidebook called "One Day Jaunts from

London." He held it open to the section on Canterbury and read aloud, "St. Peter's, a local parish church with 6th century foundations and a leper's window, is the oldest church in Canterbury, possibly the oldest church in English-speaking Christendom. It is claimed that St. Augustine preached to Queen Bertha and 10,000 Kentish men from the porch of St. Peter's in the year 596 AD and converted them to Christianity on the spot." Will whistled. "That's some preaching!"

"Yes." I said. "I do know about it. We will go there, but first I have to find this chapel. Will, I've just GOT to." I couldn't tell him why I needed to do this. What would I say? Will grimaced and he followed along with even less enthusiasm.

"We can go to St. Peter's tomorrow," I said soothingly over my shoulder, "after we've looked at this chapel. I feel so sure it's somewhere here."

Suddenly we saw someone. The first person we had come upon since turning into St. Martin's Lane. He was a tall man, almost as tall as Will, with an imposing mustache. He was pushing a lawn mower. About 65, fit-looking, he stared at us through steel-rimmed glasses, large sandy eyebrows pulled down in a puzzled frown, the huge grey-blond RAF mustache wriggling about his face with a life of its own. Then his face lit up. "You've come. You're really here!" he said with a throb in his voice. He pulled off his soiled work gloves, stepped toward me and grabbed my hand. "I've waited so long!"

Will and I exchanged glances. He thought he knew us! But the weird thing was that I also had a feeling that I had seen him before.

"Excuse me, sir," I said, gently extricating my hand. "Perhaps you've mistaken me for someone else. We just wanted to ask you if you could tell us where to find the Chapel of Bones? We heard it was down this road."

The man nodded his head and smiled. "Right. Certainly. Of course you do."

"I suppose lots of people come traipsing down this road, bothering you about it?"

"Not at all," the man said. "I can't remember the last person. I'll show it you, if you like. You'll have questions. I can answer them." He held his head as though he were listening for something. Why did he seem so familiar?

"You know, perhaps you're right. You're not exactly what I...." he said, looking puzzled. He shook his head. I barely caught his mumbled words. "Too old. And a girl?"

The man held out his hand to Will this time.

"Let me introduce myself. Name's Cooper. Algernon Cooper. I live in this pile here." He pointed to the house behind him. The lawn he had been cutting, striped with the back and forth of the mower, was like emerald velvet. A flower border running around the outside was crowded with late bronze chrysanthemums. A huge bouquet of them filled the front window of Mr. Cooper's house.

"How do you do, sir," Will said. "I'm Will Morton and this is my wife, Martha." I shook the man's hand. "I am delighted to meet you," I said. But puzzlement rather than delight was what I was feeling.

I looked straight into his eyes. They were grey with tiny sparkling glints in them. There was something about him. "Mr. Cooper, you know, I think you do look familiar to me. Do I know you from somewhere?"

He looked straight back at me and a tiny smile began to play about his lips. "I don't think Algie Cooper has ever met any young Americans before today," he said with a chuckle. He turned and began to walk down the lane. "Now come this way. We'll have a little tour."

We followed him. I was so absorbed in trying to figure out where I had seen him before, that I barely listened to his tour-guide patter, how the land all about belonged to a monastery in the middle ages and how, as a solicitor, he had needed to decipher medieval manuscripts to determine whether he could have a freehold to the property. Will was a doctoral student researching legal records of the 14th and 15th century. Medieval documents were his meat and drink. Will peppered Mr. Cooper with questions, but I just stared at the thick grey-blonde hair on the back of the man's head. As for me, I just wanted to find out as much as I could about early medieval architecture. I'd figure out whether I wanted to work on a graduate degree later.

The humming began in my head and grew louder as we walked from the pavement, onto a path through the hedges and into the woods. And a sensation of being pulled began, as though something was drawing me forward.

"Look right there," Mr. Cooper gestured toward the almost circular structure. The way the slate roof sat, like a hat on the top, made it look like something very early, pre-middle ages, maybe. It was not the shape of any of the medieval chapels I'd studied. But it was, as far as I could tell, like the building in my book. That one had been peeking out, only partly visible, from behind the ruins of a Cistercian monastery and the text had read, "14th c. Abbey with ossuary." It fit perfectly with the thesis I was pursuing, that many of the foundations of Saxon churches were actually built by Roman Christians or that the Saxons had even used the Roman temples as churches themselves. The common theory held that almost everything had been destroyed in the Saxon invasions after the retreat of the Legions, but that couldn't have been. In much of the country it took centuries for the Roman government and culture to fade away. I was seeking evidence that there was a continuity, not previously documented, in the Saxon religious structures, of Roman building materials and architectural details. I stood very still, my heart drumming in counterpoint to the humming. A stone path circled around the walls and led to the padlocked wooden door. It was a small building, no more than about 30 feet in diameter. It was at this point that I saw the ghostly images emerge of the two men carrying the stretcher.

The previous day, at my insistence, we had stopped at Rochester Cathedral on our way to Canterbury. In the crypt was part of the foundation of the original cathedral, founded in 604. Will watched me lay my hand on the wall, fingers gently stroking the stones. His eyes widened as he saw the sudden tremor course through me. But he didn't seem to hear the almost indiscernible sound, whispering or murmuring, that accompanied it.

"Do you hear something?" I had asked very softly, hopefully, taking his hand in mine. Light from the stairs leading to the nave shone down on his face, highlighting high cheekbones and slightly out-thrust jaw. He looked so handsome standing there. "Please," I thought, "share this with me."

I almost hated him when his eyes rolled up toward the crypt's arches and he shook his head. He cupped a hand to his right ear and cocked his head. "Hark!" he said, and then whispered from behind his other hand, "You have to say 'hark' in a place like this." Then in a normal tone, "I hear somebody upstairs in the nave leading a tour and talking about... something or other."

I put my hand on the foundation stone again. "When I put my hand here, I feel a sort of vibration and hear a sound, like whispering or chanting."

Not a chance. My new husband screwed up his face and shook his head. "Marti," he said, " I think you need some lunch,".

Now, as we stood before the Chapel of Bones, Will obviously noticed nothing more than that I had stumbled. Even as he reached out to keep me upright, he continued his conversation with Mr. Cooper. Cooper, however, was now looking directly at me in a speculative fashion, still with that hint of a smile. My mouth was too dry to say anything at all. I just walked forward, aware that both Mr. Cooper and Will were speaking, though the noise in my head and my heart drowned out everything else.

As I came closer to the little building, I began to notice grey, white and yellow pieces of something, not stone, perhaps shell, set into the mortar every which way, no order or pattern at all. As I looked more closely at them, I saw familiar shapes, cross-sections and long sections of what looked like human bones.

"My God," I whispered, "there really are bones stuck into the wall!"

I walked up and rubbed at the collected grime on the distorted panes of one of the windows, trying to peer into the interior. I could barely make out a small circular room. It was empty, completely empty. I could see thickly plastered walls, from which the long narrow shapes protruded. The interior diameter looked to be half that of the exterior, so the walls had to be incredibly thick.

"I can't see anything," Will said. He was looking over my shoulder at the window.

"It looks like the inside walls also are full of bones," I mumbled.

"Oh, they are!" said Mr. Cooper.

I turned to him. "Is there any way I could get into that chapel?"

"My dear Mrs. Morton, *you* can see what it is like. It's an empty dusty room. Just a lot of plaster and bones."

"How do you know? Have you been inside?" I did know that room and it wasn't empty, despite what I was seeing through the window. It had an altar and a crucifix and shelves around the walls with bones on them. But how could I know that? Maybe if I got inside, I could figure it out.

"Marti is an architectural historian, you see," Will said.

"Ah yes, that explains it." And Mr. Cooper looked at me with one eyebrow raised.

He turned back to the chapel and resumed his lecture as though we had not just had that exchange.

"The bones were set into the walls and the plaster put over them, layer after layer, during the plague in the 14th cen…" I could hear his voice growing fainter and fainter.

"Are you feeling quite well, my dear?" I barely heard Mr. Cooper speaking. I was vaguely aware of Will looking at me in alarm as I sank to my knees and then passed out completely.

Just before I slipped into the mists of unconsciousness, I saw another image. A young, lean, clean-shaven monk, looking very much like Mr. Cooper, walking in a line of monks out of a gate tower and along the city wall, each of them carrying a lit candle and all of them chanting.

When I came to, I was cradled in Will's arms. I could hear Mr. Cooper from a distance away, saying, "I think she's coming round." I opened my eyes and saw him lighting his pipe, watching me from behind a puff of smoke. Will was rubbing my wrists and saying, "Marti, wake up. Marti what happened?"

Pulling me to a sitting position, Will gently pushed my head between my knees until all feeling of dizziness passed. With an arm firmly around my back, he helped me to stand up. I was still a bit shaky.

"I'm okay, Will," I said. "Just the excitement."

Mr. Cooper nodded his head. "Ah, yes," he said, "it would be exciting, wouldn't it?

He turned from us. "Look, I have to get back to my mowing. If that lawn isn't all cut by the time my dear wife comes back from her marketing, I'll hear about it. Look around all you like." He winked at me and started back down the path.

For an instant though, as he was disappearing through the roof-high shrubs, I saw him wearing a long brown robe, a rope tied around the waist. Frozen to the spot for a moment, I then ran wordlessly after him, as he disappeared down the tree-lined path.

"Marti, where are you going?" Will called.

I caught up to Mr. Cooper just after he had resumed mowing. He turned and looked at me, without any recognition, a totally unremarkable middle-aged twentieth century man in cotton pants and a striped polo shirt.

"Well, hello there," he said. "Are you looking for something?"

Will caught up to me. "But, Mr. Cooper..." he began. I elbowed Will in the ribs gently and pulled him along. "No thank you, sir," I said over my shoulder, and we walked, as quickly as we could, out of the lane.

"Is he nuts, or what?" Will was shaking his head. I shrugged because I couldn't figure out how to answer him.

I wasn't completely sure what had just happened, but it was clear that the man we had just left behind had no awareness at all of having seen us before. But now Will had actually experienced one of the weird phenomena that had been present in my life since I was very small. Had he seen Mr. Cooper turn into a monk? I was pretty sure that the Mr. Cooper who had shown us the Chapel was someone else entirely from the man who was just now mowing the lawn. How could I convince Will about this when I didn't understand it myself? How could I even broach the subject?

2
Meeting Will 1948

I RAN UP the stairs to the classroom building. It was September, 1948, my second year at Barnard College at Columbia and the first day of classes. The political campaign for President was heating up, and everywhere there were tables and posters touting support for Truman, Dewey and Henry Wallace. I hadn't yet decided between Truman or Wallace. Supporting Wallace, the Progressive Party candidate, would be the most dramatic position I could take to counter my father's segregationist, Dixiecrat views.

I had I signed up for a course in medieval history, having just decided that would be my major. I was sure that my attraction to the buildings, ruins, churches, cottages that I knew so well from my book on England was influenced by my strange ability to see and know people and events from the past. When I looked at my book, I could feel the roughness of the stone, the graininess of the carvings, almost taste the musty air. My strange ability would not seem weird if I studied ancient buildings and the people who lived in them.

I tapped firmly at the classroom door before opening it. Through tall windows on one side of the room I could see the steps of Butler Library, with a colorful parade of dozens of students going up and down. Sitting in front of the windows was a tall skinny guy leaning back in a chair with a desk-arm, tilted so that only the back two legs were on the floor. He was wearing chino slacks and a white shirt with the sleeves rolled halfway up his arms, and a tie loosened and hanging far below his neck. He was working on a crossword in a newspaper folded on the desk-arm and seemed to be the one in charge, since his chair sat in solitary command facing a semi-circle of such chairs. Six other students were already seated, looking at their notebooks or chatting softly. No one looked up when I opened the door. "Excuse me." I cleared my throat, straightened up as tall as I could, and spoke a bit louder, "Is this where Medieval History is meeting?" The leader looked up from his newspaper as I entered. He grinned at me and said, "Yup, but there's this test for admission." He looked down again, his pencil poised in mid air. "What's a nine-letter word beginning with A and ending in INE, the definition is the first Christian Saint in England. Argentine would fit, but I've never heard of a St. Argentine, and Augustine was in North Africa, not England." The other students looked up, broke into smiles and watched me.

I shook my head. I was pleased to start by showing off a little. I couldn't help liking this discussion leader already. And if there was a so-called test for admission, I was glad to know that I would pass.

"You're talking about Augustine of Hippo in North Africa. There's another saint of the same spelling pronounced 'AuGUStin.' He was about two hundred years after the one in Hippo and he was sent to convert the people of Kent, England."

"Oh excellent. Thanks." He let the chair bang down onto to four feet and leaned forward to scribble the missing letters.

"So, I passed?"

"You not only passed, but you can finish this crossword, if you want." He handed me the paper and pulled a notebook out of his book bag. He looked around at the class and in a slightly louder voice announced, "This is the workshop section of Medieval History 201. I'm Will Morton. I'm the graduate assistant, and I'm going to lead this class." He looked directly at me again and asked, "And you are?" His pencil was poised above the notebook.

"Martha. Martha Davis. How do you do."

We shook hands and I sat down in a chair in the semicircle, right in the middle directly opposite him. I instantly regretted that I had taken a seat in far too prominent a place.

It's true that he was awfully cute, but it unnerved me that he kept glancing at me with one eyebrow raised and a slight upturn of his lips, as he handed out the syllabus and reading list. He described the format for the weekly oral presentations we were expected to offer as though I were the only person in the class. I could feel that I was blushing. Will told me much later that he thought the heightened color only made me more adorable, but at the time I was annoyed that this failing of mine ruined the self-assured manner I yearned to present.

I would have vehemently denied that I was trying to see him outside of class, but the next day I found I had to go to his office to get a permission slip for the library. His office door was open and he was again sitting leaning back on his desk chair with his feet up on the desk. Two charts of numbers were tacked up on a bulletin board in front of him and he was making notes on a legal-sized yellow pad.

"Excuse me. May I interrupt you for a moment?" I really didn't know how much deference was due to graduate assistants.

Will turned around, letting the front legs of his chair fall back to the floor. He smiled at me, hopped up and moved a bunch of books off the only other chair in the room, gestured for me to sit and said, "Miss Martha Davis, come in. Have a seat. I've been wanting to ask you about this Chesapeake Bay community you come from. I don't think I've ever met anyone from there before. Can you really eat all the crab meat that you want?"

"How did you know I'm from...? Oh, you must have looked me up. I've never eaten much crab, myself. We call it "crab" not crab "meat." They're scavengers, you know." I decided he was not due much deference at all. "The Bay has a lot better eating than that."

"Mmm," He looked at me with a slight smile and half-closed eyes. "You'll have to introduce me to some of those good things and tell me all about life on 'the Bay'?"

This man was flirting with me! I tried to think what to say in response. I looked at him and bit my lips while trying to summon the right level of casual disinterest.

"There's shad. And wonderful oysters. So what did you want to know?" I asked.

"Everything. But I tell you what. I need a break, let's go across the street and have some coffee."

"Is it allowed for graduate students to fraternize with undergraduates?" I said in a smart alecky way. I felt my cheeks grow stiff. What had we just said to one another? He was flirting with me. But was I leading him on? I could just hear my mother's parting advice, "And Martha, you must never let a man you are not engaged to take liberties with you. Be very careful, dear." I couldn't believe her! I was sorely tempted to ask her, "So it's alright for a man who is RELATED to me?" but I just wanted to get on the train.

Will was pushing in his chair and reaching for his jacket. He did not see my face resume its guarded expression.

He signed my library permission slip, closed his office door, put his hand on my elbow and led me across Broadway. I tried to detach myself from my arm, holding my elbow out at right angles to my side so that Will was forced to walk more than a foot away from me. How many liberties could he take in the Chockful o' Nuts? We sat on stools at the counter. Mirrors on all the walls allowed me to see our faces next to one another, and at the same time, our two backs. Everyone in the restaurant was reflected over and over. A bored-looking counterman slapped a paper napkin down in front of each of us and said, "Yeah, what'llyahave?" Will spun around on his seat. "Let's see, what'll we have? Isn't there some movie with Fred Astaire or Gene Kelly, where the guy tap dances while spinning from stool to stool in a lunch counter? I've always wanted to do that."

"Please don't," I murmured, staring fixedly at the menu printed on the mirror.

Will ordered a cup of coffee and I decided on a chocolate milkshake. We both ordered whole wheat donuts. "I feel less sinful when the donut is made from whole wheat," I told him.

"I don't know, young woman. That is pretty sinful! What other debaucheries do you engage in? Bringing library books back late? Leaving the light on in the closet? Not writing home every Saturday?"

I shook my head. "Nothing worse than donuts, I'm afraid."

"OK, tell me what it's like where you came from."

So I told him about our town, the two-hundred-year-old house I grew up in. "We live right on Chesapeake Bay. I learned to swim and to canoe and kayak when I was very little." Will listened intently as though I were telling him about the most fascinating place on earth. His eyes never left my face. He asked intelligent, serious questions. What was the population? Were most people Democrats? What was the chief economic activity? What churches were there? What sort of town government? He wasn't joking now. I amazed myself that I even knew the answers to some of his questions.

"Well, it's not the most cosmopolitan place in the world." I concluded after my third donut. "And if I keep eating like this, I'll sink my canoe when I get back there."

Despite my feeling of vulnerability at kidding around with a man, it had been about as unthreatening as it could be. But afterwards I found myself picturing him over and over in his little office leaning back in a chair with only two legs on the floor.

A few days later I emerged with a crowd of other students from an English Lit. Class and there he was, lounging against the beige corridor wall, with one knee bent and his foot resting against the baseboard. I had the distinct impression that he had been waiting for me, when he looked up from his newspaper, placed his foot back on the floor, and said, "Hi there, Martha Elizabeth Davis – wow, that's too much name. Don't you have a nickname?"

"Well, my real name is actually Martha Elizabeth Anne Priscilla Charlotte Davis. My mother has exactly the same name except hers begins Elizabeth Martha. That's why I prefer to be called Marti."

"Ok, Marti it is. So have you had a chance to go over to Riverside Park and watch the sun go down over the Palisades?"

I shook my head. "Is that one of the recommended activities?"

"Let me be the first to show it to you."

I quickly ran through the proprieties in my mind. I had been in the park, of course, but not at sunset. It, like the coffee shop, would be full of people and I should be able to keep to the paths. He really seemed like a decent guy.

We crossed Riverside and walked into the park. A huge red sun, just emerging from dark clouds, was hanging over the Palisades. Its beams formed an orange path right across the river to where we were standing. I could hear the muted roar of traffic below on the West Side Highway, but in the park it was quiet enough for the singing of homecoming birds to be the main sound. The leaves had mostly fallen from the trees, and great drifts of them, golden, red, and pale green, blanketed the grass and the walks. There was a crisp, yeasty smell. We walked along side by side, not talking, just scuffling our feet in the leaf-piles, and then Will scooped up a large pile of them and dropped them on my head.

"Oh, you!" I shouted, "I'll get you for that." I jumped up on a bench to throw a handful of leaves over his head, but he was too tall and too agile. He sprinted away, laughing as I chased him.

As I caught up to him, he turned and I threw my armload of leaves at his face. "Oh yeah!" he said, and tossed more leaves at me. We chased each other up and down the path, feinting and darting from side to side, but neither of us succeeded in getting many leaves on the other. Until he collapsed on a bench and I dumped a last handful on his head. "Gotcha!" I crowed and then fell onto the bench next to him. Both of us were breathing hard and I felt as though the pulses in my temples were about to thump right out of my head. I crossed my arms over my belly and curled over so that my head was approaching my knees and took long even breaths to calm myself. Will put his hand on my shoulder. "Are you ok?" he asked. I nodded, feeling confused and not knowing what to do with my confusion. Should I get up and run away or tell him off for, for… what? Will reached out and picked a leaf out of my hair and held it up to me. I took it and held it and rubbed it between my thumb and index finger. I put it into my pocket. Will took my hand in his. I pulled it away and put both hands into my armpits.

"Marti, please give me your hand," he said very softly. I shook my head which was still suspended slightly above my knees. "Please," he said. Slowly, tentatively, I pulled my hand out and allowed him to take it, looking sideways at him from under my bent head. He turned it over so that my palm was exposed and with the nail of his index finger, he gently traced along the lines. I shivered. Then he lifted my hand to his lips and placed a kiss in the middle of my palm. I pulled my hand away and put it into my pocket. I couldn't look at him. I didn't know what to say. I felt as though my blood was carbonated. I had never before had anyone kiss my palm.

I swallowed. I spoke in a barely audible voice to my right loafer, "I wish you wouldn't do that."

I turned to him. Will was smiling broadly at me. My heart was beating as though it would jump out of my chest, but I forced my voice to stay calm and low, "I don't know how I can take you seriously as a graduate assistant when you act like such a kid." I struggled not to grin back at him, but my lips had a mind of their own. "And you're so fresh! You're supposed to set an example for us undergraduates." A giggle burst out, but I wrestled my mouth back into a stern expression.

"I just did," he too composed his features into a serious expression and cleared his throat several times. "I'm giving you an object lesson called, 'Don't take yourself too seriously. Don't work too hard. Stop and get some physical activity!" An impish look broke through again, "The kiss on the hand was just thrown in for extra credit." I shot him a glance out of half-closed eyes and then stood up, whirled around like a dancer on a music box, curtsied to him, and started back to campus.

Later that evening as I tried to concentrate on my reading, amusement tickled a place just under my ribs and then bubbled up through my body, erupting as a giggle. I took the little leaf out of my pocket and put it into my book as a place marker. I put the book on the quilt at the foot of my bed and stretched my arms over my head, closed my eyes and let a wide, happy smile crinkle my cheeks. I could feel the dizzying deliciousness of us chasing each other. My hand still tingled where it had been kissed.

3
A Strange Ability 1932 - 1952

MY MEMORIES OF my strange ability to see people and scenes that were invisible to others all blur together, but the first one I really remember must have been when I was about three.

Too big for a high chair, I sat on two pillows at the dining room table, putting one piece of my cut-up canned peaches at a time onto my spoon, carefully licking my fingers and then, just as carefully spooning the piece of peach into my mouth. I watched the woman move across the dining room. She was dressed like one of the pictures in my Mother Goose book, a wimple on her head, a laced up bodice, a long dark skirt. I spent so much time staring at the pictures in that book, pretending I was in them, dreaming about them, that there was nothing strange to me about her appearance. But in this case I could see right through her. She had come in through the wall, seemed to float through the sideboard and the big mahogany table and right out through the opposite wall.

"Mama," I said, licking the peach juice off my spoon and pointing toward the wall, "Who was that lady?"

My mother looked up from her newspaper.

"What lady, Martha?" She looked at the wall where I was pointing.

"That see-through lady walked right through that wall."

She drew in her breath sharply and grabbed my chin so that my face was just a few inches from hers. "Martha," she said, "If you tell another fib like that, I will have to spank you. Hard!"

I looked down at my bowl and dipped my finger in the juice. I put my finger in my mouth and sucked on it. Apparitions like that continued to appear throughout my childhood, but I knew better than to mention them.

When I was thirteen, during World War II, the postman brought a package. It was covered with stamps that had pictures of King George VI of England. It was sent to me by my cousin who was stationed there, waiting for the invasion of France to begin.

I tore off the wrappings and opened the book, *The Country Life Picture Book of Britain,* a collection of photographs of scenic places. I felt as though my fingers had suddenly become electric. If I touched anything, I would spark. The pages shouted to me. My hand vibrated as I opened the cover.

I turned the first page and looked at the photo of Plumpton Manor in Sussex with the South Downs rising steeply behind it. All at once I found myself running into the scene across the uplands and meadows above the house. My hair was blown as I looked down upon the huge, half-timbered building. Then I was back, the book still in my hand. I looked at the picture again and suddenly only one part of the building could be seen, just the part that I now know existed in the 14th century, and in front of it stood the village of Ramsgate Overbrook, with the local village court in session. And once again I was in the scene, approaching it along the muddy path.

I quickly became as devoted to this book as I had been to the nursery rhymes. As I turned the pages, I came upon a picture of the gate that led into the Canterbury Cathedral close. I knew that just up the street, out of the picture, would be that tower in the city wall. I laughed at myself. How could I possibly know this? I had never been to

Canterbury. Hardly ever been out of Cambridge, Maryland until I went to college.

I devoured every page of the book. I pored over it again and again, carried it with me everywhere, each night focussed on a new page, and for a few moments I would actually walk in these places. I carried the book's pictures in my mind and they became mixed with the other images, the ones that came to me in quiet moments and before I fell asleep. I saw people dressed in clothing of earlier times, tunics and woolen hose, kirtles and bodices, knee breeches, stove pipe hats. I heard distant sounds, as though many people were speaking too far away to be heard. The pictures in the book were black and white, but the scenes in my mind were always in color.

I knew, though I tried to pretend otherwise, that my obsession with the book, with finding the real physical places in it, had been behind my consuming need to go to England, and even to some degree behind my agreeing to marry Will. Ever since I had gotten the book I had been feeling, with constantly increasing intensity, that I had to get to England. There was something I had to find.

And something I had to do!

Now, as we walked out of St. Martin's Lane, Will was still shaking his head over the strange way Mr. Cooper had reacted.

"What kind of mental condition leads to not remembering something that happened five minutes before?"

But I just said, "We've got to get back to the Youth Hostel. I need to change my shoes. My feet are killing me." I wanted to pore over the book again.

I sat on my bunk in the women's section of the hostel and pulled it out of my backpack. It opened automatically to what was for me the most compelling place. As I often did, I immediately entered the picture on the page. I was walking toward the picturesque ruins of St. Martin's Abbey just outside the walls of Canterbury. The roofless structure with its Norman tower rose up from the water meadows surrounding it. As

I approached it, the Abbey became whole again, glass restored to the lower parts of the vaulted windows, and men wearing brown woolen robes marched, two by two, along the path leading to the cloister. One of them turned back to look at me, his clear grey eyes staring at me as though he knew me well. It was Mr. Cooper, or rather the monk I had seen before fainting. He beckoned to me. It had never happened before that one of my images invited me into the scene. "Thank God!" he murmured and reached out to squeeze my shoulder, as I fell into the line next to him. The monks were chanting as they repeated the paternoster. For a brief time I walked with them, but then I dozed off and the book fell from my hands...

4
Anselm 1331

BROTHER DAVID, THE chronicler, placed the oil lamp on the table where 12-year-old Anselm sat brushing scarlet into the huge initial letter "A" on the vellum sheet before him. He patted the boy's shoulder and said, "There is no need for you to risk becoming blind before your time."

The late November afternoon had grown dark and the wind howled around the high, gothic windows in the scriptorium. Only the lower parts of the windows were glazed, to keep the rain and snow off the manuscripts, those being prepared, and even more important, those being preserved from earlier times.

Brother David was saying something to Anselm. The boy shook his head and forced himself to focus on the monk's words.

"I crave your pardon, Brother, I was lost in my thoughts."

"The Abbot wishes to see you in his closet. He wants to examine your work." David rolled up the vellum and carefully tied a linen cord around it. He placed it in the hand of the boy. "Be sure to wash your face and hands before you go to him."

Anselm hunched his shoulders, like one avoiding a blow. When David turned back from removing a sheepskin from its stretcher, Anselm had still not moved. "Go on, child. The Abbot is waiting. It won't do to be too long in getting there."

Anselm held out the rolled vellum toward David. "Please, Brother, could you not show it to him for me?"

"Anselm, what is wrong with you? You're being honored by the Abbot's attention. I've been praying that he would take an interest and see how skilled you've become at both the lettering and the illuminations. Surely you realize my greatest wish is that when you've taken your vows, you will officially be my assistant here, and be appointed chronicler in my place when I am gone."

Anselm's head shot up and he looked at David. He could feel his lips begin to quiver. "Gone? Dear Brother, where are you going?" Brother David had been Anselm's mother and father since he was found in a blizzard, a tiny babe wrapped in a sling at his dead mother's breast.

Brother David looked fondly at the boy. "You are growing so tall, Anselm," he said, "and your face is no longer round as an apple." David patted Anselm's cheek. "Oh, what has happened to my boy child? He will soon be a man, alas." Then his manner became grave.

"Anselm, my eyes see less with each passing day. God has blessed me with the work of recording St. Martin's history, of telling again the holy stories, and of caring for our precious library. I've rejoiced each day to do such a service for Him. But soon someone else will have to do it, and I would like it to be you." He held Anselm's face up and looked into his eyes.

"Go to the Abbot, now, my child. We will talk more of these matters when the time comes."

Anselm took up the rolled vellum and started slowly down the narrow circular stairs. It was too dark to see where he was going. The stone walls were cold and the dampness felt to his hand like tears as he braced himself against them. He carefully placed one foot after the other on the triangular stone steps. Why couldn't Brother David see the danger Anselm knew awaited him?

His temples throbbed as he forced his foot downward. His shaking made it particularly difficult to keep his balance. What if he ran away?

He stopped and tried to force himself to breathe deeply, to no avail. His foot searched for the next step. Where could he hide? There were many places in the monastery where few ever went. The granary, perhaps? He connected with a step and felt for the next one. If he couldn't be found for a while, maybe the Abbot would forget about him. He looked wildly around as his feet reached the lantern-lit main floor of the building.

Then he smelled the aromas from the kitchens and suddenly felt less panicked. It was almost time for the evening meal. He had seen the kitchen monks bringing in a large basket of bruised apples fallen from the trees. An apple tart might be part of the meal. Such treats were usually saved for feast days, but there'd been a frost and he'd heard one of the cooks say that the dropped apples would rot if not used quickly. If he reported to the Abbot's study right now, there would only be a few minutes until the bells rang calling them to vespers and to the refectory.

He knocked on the door of the study, though his heart still thumped, his breath still shallow, and his voice, never quite reliable these days, quavered, first high-pitched and then emerging from his throat in a deep baritone.

"You wished to see me, Your Grace?"

Abbot Godwin was grey, very tall and thin, with broad, powerful shoulders. He sat, leaning on his desk with two large white outstretched hands. He looked at Anselm, his eyes almost closed, his mouth turned down in a look of great sternness. "Close the door behind you," he said, his voice the rasping sound Anselm remembered well. Anselm resisted a powerful urge to run out. He carefully pulled the door to, pushing down on the large latch until it was caught tight.

The Abbot pushed back from his writing table and motioned the boy to him. The room was warm, almost stifling, with its thick carpet and roaring fire. "Show me your work," he demanded. Anselm trembled and felt as though he'd faint, but he placed the vellum on the table between them. "Open it." Anselm unrolled the page and leaned forward to hold it down so the huge illuminated "A" faced the man. The letter was made of tendrils and blossoms, small red fruit, and had a leering serpent curling around the cross bar. It was followed by the smaller fine careful letters "d-a-m" in black ink.

"Which part of this is your work?" the Abbot's eyes were completely open now, and he looked carefully at the letters, then up at Anselm.

"Brother David drew the outline of the illuminated letter and of the foliage. I did the color and drew the serpent and the blossoms and I did the letters that follow, if you please, Your Grace."

"This is fine work, lad. Brother David has taught you well." He traced his finger down the whole of the snake's body. "It seems you know much about the serpent, boy," the Abbot said and he coughed a laugh. Half closing his eyes again, he motioned to the boy to come around the table to him.

When Anselm was in touching distance, the Abbot put his hands around the boy's waist and drew him closer, holding him tightly between his powerful thighs. He closed his eyes completely and ran his hands over the Anselm's flanks and then around his hips to his groin, where he grabbed for his penis and scrotum, holding them firmly through the rough cloth of the covering garments. To his horror, Anselm felt his penis stiffen, and he let out a gasp. The Abbot, his eyes still closed, smiled. He opened them again and released the boy.

Anselm's blood still pounded in his ears and his breath came in short panting gasps. The bell calling them to vespers began to ring and the Abbot said, "Go." Then added, "Leave the vellum here."

Anselm ran to the corridor outside the refectory and took his place in the file of chanting monks preparing to go to into the chapel. He stood, feeling his face burning and his hands freezing, his stomach turning over so that bitter juices came up into his mouth. He clamped his mouth shut to keep from retching.

The memory of a time, never very far from his mind, came flooding back, of his face being pressed down and almost smothered in a pillow, the rasping voice telling him to lie still, while something was forced, horribly, painfully, into him from behind. He had been sick for days afterwards, his bowels troubling him for many weeks. Now suddenly he bolted out of the line of monks and ran outside to vomit.

5
Midnight Journey 1952

THE BOOK FALLING from my sleep-relaxed hand woke me to the realization that I was still lying, fully clothed, on my youth hostel bed. I got undressed and climbed into my sleeping bag. I lay completely still listening to the breathing of the other sleepers in the women's dormitory, holding my breath, only one eye peeking out of my sleeping bag. I wished Will were with me.

It was the practice of the hosteling association for men to sleep in a male dormitory and women in the female section, with no provision for married couples. As he had kissed me good night on the stairs leading to the upper floors, I said, "I'm feeling scared, Will. I wish we were going to be together." He had leaned down and kissed my neck. "Hey, babe, if anything scary comes at you, just point your finger at it and say, 'Go away!' And they have to do it. It's in the spooky-things-union contract." I stood on tiptoes to reach his lips and hugged him as hard as I could. "And in which of your documents did you read this goofy contract?" I asked, and we both laughed, hoisted our back packs and went our separate ways.

Now a full moon was shining into the window, but at the same time, little tendrils of fog were also creeping in, then more and more until, out of the fog coming into the room, a larger, denser form emerged and wafted in through the window. It was a human form, in a long dark hooded garment. It moved toward my bed, floating a bit above the floor, utterly without a sound. A hand reached out toward me, then abruptly moved up and pushed the hood off its head. Against the light from the window, I could see a man's face, and drew in my breath. His hand moved to his mouth in that ages-old gesture of quiet, his index finger raised upward across his lips.

He sat down next to my bunk, though there was nothing there to sit on, and looked directly at me. His face was familiar. I knew him. It was Mr. Cooper, but clean shaven, and thinner, younger-looking. I had seen him several times when I entered the pictures in my book.

"Who are you." I asked, then realized that I had not in fact spoken, only thought the words.

"I am Anselm. I become Cooper when it suits me. I followed the rule of the blessed Benedict, though I am no longer in this life." Only my mind apprehended his words, but I knew he had a deep and quiet voice. Much more serious than Mr. Cooper.

"We are speaking in our minds," I observed with amazement.

"We can do this only when it is absolutely necessary," he replied.

I thought about this for a moment, then realized that it was probably the presence of the other sleepers that made it necessary.

"You mean you are no longer a monk?"

"No, I mean that I ceased to live as others live over six hundred years ago, as you reckon time. I can sometimes become other people when I need to."

There was no time to ask about that remarkable statement.

The mists were swirling in the room, and in them I began to make out miniature farm fields and a walled community, with a circular chapel and other stone buildings within the walls, much like an aerial view from my book. A line of monks (were they the same ones I had walked with before?) walked down the lane from a burial ground that surrounded the chapel at one side of the compound.

The apparition, Mr. Cooper, Anselm or whoever he was, reached out for my hand. I didn't hesitate. I grasped his outstretched palm, and as mists swirled around, my body lifted from the bed, and instantly I was walking in the file of monks down the lane. I looked for Anselm and saw him walking far down the line. My right arm supported something that leaned on my shoulder, an iron shovel, dirt-encrusted and very heavy. I staggered under the weight of it, tripping and falling out of line, coming down heavily on my knees. There was a searing feeling and I looked down and saw blood begin to seep from the left knee of my baggy hose. A tall, bearded man grabbed my arm from behind me and helped me regain my footing. He came alongside and continued to keep a hand under my bent elbow.

"It's all right, lad," he said quietly to me. "You'll soon be able to rest and eat your porridge. You're too young for such hard work, but we need every live body we can find to put away the dead ones. In my day, a novice was the younger son of one of the best families, respectful, dignified. Now the only riches the novices bring us are the promise of strong backs."

My head buzzed. I wished he'd be quiet so I could try to figure out what was happening. Where was Anselm? And why did this man call me "lad?" Was this a dream? I was about to say, "But, I'm not a..." When something made me look down at my chest under a dirty, wool tunic. I had always been pleased with my full round breasts on my boy-slim body, but now I could see my chest was as flat as a board, and the sagging, bloody hose on my legs had a tied-on flap over the pubic area. With my free hand I reached up to my head and found under the pointy hood, that my scalp was shaved clean. My long red braid was gone.

While I was assessing myself, we continued to trudge along and now turned into a gateway leading to the main entrance courtyard of the monastery. Anselm, at the far end of the courtyard, turned to look for me. When he saw me, he nodded and entered one of the buildings. All around, the men threw down the tools they had been carrying, stretching and scratching themselves. They wandered over to a walled-off section, its purpose easily identified by the stench, and proceeded to relieve themselves. Hesitating only for a second, I followed, suddenly aware of my own need, and untying the flap on my hose, I reached in and gingerly touched something totally alien. "Oh my God," I mumbled to myself. "This had better be a dream." But then I took hold of this newly-acquired organ, and followed suit.

"Ha, wait until I tell Will about this!" I mumbled to myself and then laughed out loud. As I fumbled with the strings on the flap, I had a feeling that someone was watching me.

A short fat monk came forward. "What is so funny, youngster?" he asked, as he grabbed my hands with one of his own, preventing me from closing my garments. The other men had left quickly, and I realized that I was all alone in this walled off place with this monk. He stood behind me, holding my two hands tightly in one of his, as he reached around and began to stroke my penis while he put his lips and tongue to my ear. I shuddered and shoved my sharp elbows back with all my might, leaning first front and then back, as I tried to throw him off balance. Pulling one hand free, I pointed a finger at him and screamed, "go away!" The fat monk disappeared. In the blink of an eye, Anselm appeared. He patted my arm and said quietly, "Yes. You'll do very well."

The next instant, my heart still beating wildly and tears streaming down my face, I was back in the sleeping bag, my long braid imprisoned under one shoulder. I could feel the burning of the place on my knee. The early sunlight could be seen in the window, trying to break through the clouds of a light rain.

6
The Plague Begins 1349

ANSELM TRIED TO catch his breath as he watched, out of a corner of his eye, a rat creeping along the refectory wall. Despite his having run there with the others when the unexpected bell began to toll, Anselm's mind was still preoccupied with the parchment he had been working on in the library. Since he had taken Brother David's place as the monastery's chronicler and chief illuminator, he had quickly come to think of each one of the hundreds of folios and scrolls as his own books. Leaning over the drawing of the gathered disciples, Anselm had been using a tiny brush with one stiff bristle to paint the fine gold embroidery on the hem of St. Peter's intensely blue robe. In his mind he was holding the thick rich fabric, embroidering it with the gold thread. Now, seated in the refectory, his arm and shoulder ached with the strain of keeping the line of gold absolutely controlled. He rubbed his face and his eyes and rolled his shoulders forward and backward. He tried to force himself to concentrate on his surroundings.

The monks had all run in response to the unusual tolling, each pausing at the door to genuflect to the statue of Our Lord on the wall above the high table, then joining his brothers at the lesser tables. As each man's panting subsided, the room became totally silent.

He tried to think about what this new abbot might be about to tell them, but his mind kept returning to the mayflowers he planned to draw on the border of the page. If he watered down the ground cochineal just enough, he might achieve a pink that was close to the real flower. He shook himself and again tried to focus on the abbot.

Godwin, the terrible abbot of Anselm's childhood, had simply disappeared. One afternoon his groom saddled the abbot's horse, but was told nothing about where his lord was going. He had ridden out of the monastery gate alone and did not return. The brothers divided themselves into those who would search and question in the neighborhood and those who would sit quietly and pray. After two days of fruitless effort by the monks, a farmer came to the gate leading the abbot's horse, muddy and bedraggled, its stirrups torn away and its saddle hanging askew. The beast had been wandering in the fields, grazing where it wanted. The farmer, recognizing the monastery's emblem on the saddle, led it home, but had seen no trace of its master. There had been great turmoil and even greater speculation in the monastery. Anselm said the obligatory prayers for the abbot's safe return and eventually for his soul, but his heart was not in it.

Now he was distracted by the rat. Those beasts were getting far too bold. One learned to live with the nasty things. He wriggled his toes, bare in the worn sandals, so as to discourage the rodent from thinking here was something to nibble.

Walter was the latest in the parade of abbots who served after Godwin. The brothers were wary of him since they were still getting to know him. It was highly unusual for him to call them to the refectory, since breakfast was long over. Each monk ran from his work when the summoning bell began to ring, still wearing the sweat-stained robes covered with the mark of his work. The gardening monks, their robes hoisted up, revealed the soil on their legs. The butchering monks were covered with blood and fat. The baking monk had flour in his hair and drying dough on his fingers. And Anselm had ink and colored pigment staining his hands.

The monks sat with bowed heads, waiting while the abbot stared at them, looking from one to another for what seemed an endless time. Anselm, sitting at the table farthest from the dais, could see the shaved heads of his brothers in several rows before him. The dust motes floated in the morning light that came through the open windows, then disappeared as the sun moved relentlessly across the floor.

Faintly, through the open windows, he could hear the creaking hinges of the gate beyond the cloister and then voices, one high-pitched and pleading, and one alarmed and shouting.

Just when the still congregation of men began to wriggle on their stools, trying to relieve the weight on their buttocks and the cramps in their shoulders, the abbot began to speak toward the arches of the far wall, quietly at first as though he were speaking to someone else rather than to the waiting monks.

"I am shocked!" the abbot said, turning and looking directly at them, one by one. "You should be ashamed! What sinful laxness I find in just my brief tenure here!" He paused and clasped his hands as though about to pray, then thought better of it and held his hands out to the men. "A beggar, almost naked, clothed in pitiful rags came to our gate last week. 'Help me, I am freezing. For Jesu's sake give me something warm.' I could hear him say it through my window. I saw two brothers walk by the gate. Did they stop to clothe him? No. They walked right by him.

"Every day the hungry gather for their bread. One of them might be the Savior himself. But you throw dry crusts into a trough to make them eat like pigs, and you walk away complaining that the flour from which your bread is baked is not ground finely enough."

The abbot's voice grew louder.

"Look to your feet. Are they bare?" He held out one of his own sandaled feet, his hairy toes visible. "This is what is prescribed by Saint Benedict. But many of you wear boots with the fur left on the insides. You eat too much. You sleep too much. I see how you mistreat the lay workers. Yes, don't think I don't see it. I heard a brother cursing and beating a carpenter because his measurement of a board was too long. Look at the holes in the roof! The rain pours right into this room. This is God's own house and you have neglected it."

That isn't all we have neglected, Anselm thought to himself. *No one does anything about our dirty little secret.* He was momentarily flooded with the recollection of something he'd seen as he came back from the privy very late one recent night. One of the brothers, his hand over the mouth of a boy who was struggling in his arms, disappeared into his cell. A wave of nausea poured over Anselm and he watched the rat even more intently. *We will be punished*, he thought. *God will not let these sins pass by.*

There was a sound of a person running from the cloister outside and the refectory door slammed open. All of the monks jumped and turned their heads toward the back of the room.

Standing at the door was the gatekeeper, a lay brother, who came into the refectory, bowed and said, "Please come, Reverend Father, something…" here the voice of this man, who rarely spoke, cracked with horror, "something terrible." Staring into the distance, as though he was still seeing the something, the man turned and walked out of the room, without looking to see if they were following him.

The abbot, followed by the community, ran after the gatekeeper, out of the main building of the monastery, through the courtyard and to the gate. There, a man on all fours on the ground was writhing with pain, retching into the dust. His tongue hung from his mouth. As the brothers crowded around, he looked up and barely whispered through his cracked lips, "Help me, for the love of God."

All of the brothers gasped and crossed themselves. All but Anselm and the abbot backed away. Anselm sat down on the ground and took the man's head in his lap. "Thy will be done, Lord," he murmured.

"Where is Brother Caritas?" The abbot peered into the crowd of men. "I am coming," the infirmarian called as he came, moving as quickly as he dared. He carried a dipper of water very carefully in his hands. He took the suffering man into his own lap and gently poured water into his mouth, drop by drop. Over his shoulder he spoke to Anselm. "Brother, quickly fetch a blanket and help me carry this poor wretch into the pilgrims' quarters." Anselm ran as quickly as he could and grabbed a blanket from the infirmary shelves and the two men lifted the sick man onto it.

"Go," the abbot ordered as the staring, murmuring brothers began to follow them, pointing toward the chapel, "pray for him." The brothers turned and filed off, bowing their heads and reciting the Paternoster as they went.

"You, Anselm, you will remain and help Brother Caritas."

"Yes, certainly, my lord." Anselm bowed his head in acquiescence. One of the young novices, Martin, also stayed behind. Anselm began to cut off the suffering man's filthy rags, while Martin fetched warm water and cloths to bathe the sick man. The boy reminded Anselm of himself at a similar age, and he tried to protect him, whenever he could. "Martin," Anselm now said gently, looking into the boy's brown eyes, "Lad, you must go now to the chapel." As Anselm started to bathe the exposed, shivering man, he saw that there were running sores under the man's arms and in his groin. Buboes: the telltale sign of plague.

7
St. Peter's 1952

I WOKE UP the next morning, well rested despite my nighttime journey. The place on my knee stung when my jeans brushed against it. The oatmeal plopped into my bowl by the hostel's cook was sticky and had too much salt in it. Will gave a running commentary on food as though he were writing copy for an ad agency. "Ladies, does your wallpaper depart from the walls in humid weather? Our multipurpose breakfast food and paper cement will fasten it for all time." Laughter and hunger made it somewhat edible and I washed it down with strong tea. It was Sunday morning, church bells pealing from all directions, as we left the hostel to hike into Canterbury. Almost at the gate of the city we found a small cafe just opening and treated ourselves to excellent coffee and freshly baked whole-meal bread. We were on our way to St. Peter's, as Will had suggested. The early-morning rain stopped and mists were rising into the watery sunshine as we walked up the Longport, the road adjacent to the ruins of St. Augustine's Abbey. The waves of what I called "oldness" radiated out at me, making me lightheaded. I had to fight against the magnetic pull that the Abbey's remains seemed to have on me. Like the Chapel of Bones, all these ancient places drew me and had something to do with why I had needed to be here. But what and why eluded me.

We passed by the mounds and rubble from the excavations of parts of the abbey that dated to the sixth century, and this was making my head swim as I placed one foot after the other. *I will not faint* I told myself, digging my fingernails into my palms and forcing myself to blend the humming in my head into the bee-noises from the rosebushes along the sidewalk.

I drew a deep breath and stopped and pointed to the excavations of the Abbey's foundations. "Will, do you remember the first time we met at Columbia?" Will nodded. "And you were working on a double crostic and needed a nine letter word that meant the first Christian missionary in England?"

Will nodded again. "How could I forget? The late afternoon sun was coming in the window and made your hair look like burning copper." He reached over and pushed a strand of hair off my forehead. "I couldn't take my eyes off you. And right at that moment I knew..." His voice faded away and he looked off into the distance. Then he swallowed and gave me a mischievous look. "And you were flaunting your erudition. 'It's not Augustine of Hippo but another one,'" he mimicked an English school-teacher with a high-pitched voice, "This one was later. Blah, blah. His name is usually pronounced 'Au-GUST-in.' "

"Quite right," I said in the same accent. "Well this is the Abbey that he founded."

I did not repeat my theory, a scholarly bone of contention between us, that many of the still-standing churches with parts from the Saxon period were actually built originally as Pagan temples. Will only believed what he could find documents to verify, whereas I felt I could establish my theory by archeological study of the materials used.

Will took my hand and squeezed it. "Wouldn't you love to help with the dig? We could spend some time here." It was a generous gesture, I knew that.

"Y-yes," I stuttered, "it was on my list of things I need to do." I was not ready to tell him why I needed to do these things. I squeezed his hand back. Still feeling light-headed, I barely got the words out, but Will didn't seem to notice.

A row of tiny cottages made of the ever-present brick, built as almshouses in the 16th century, stood on the opposite side of the road. Each was wide enough for a door and one window and appeared to be about twice as deep as it was wide. A single, tall chimney-pot punctuated the roof above each one. "I think people are still living in those houses," Will said. "Can you imagine raising kids in them? They probably have to sleep and eat in layers."

We turned left at the beginning of St. Peter's Hill and walked up a narrow lane with a meadow full of sheep on one side. The other side had more tiny cottages, a bit wider than those we had just seen and two stories high. The smell of poverty, overcooked cabbage and unwashed interiors, came floating out of them. A toothless old woman smoking the barest end of a cigarette, squinting from the smoke, sat on a doorstep watching some children playing in the road. We called good morning to her, but she just stared at us. We narrowly missed being run down by a pink-cheeked boy on a scooter, pushing furiously with one foot, being chased by a small girl in a navy blue school uniform. We peered under a car up on jacks to ask a man lying on his back if this was the way to St. Peter's. The man, his face covered with grease, stuck his head out and grinned at me. "Sorry, luv, they don't do weddings on Sundays, an'anyways, yer outaluck. I'm already married." He gave a braying laugh. "And you've missed the morning service."

I smiled back at him. "We just want to see the church."

"Well it's right up there, through that little gate."

Then we saw, beyond a low stone wall just where the road curved to the right, a lych-gate and beyond it some huge ancient trees. Sitting at the top of a hilly little graveyard was a small church built of rounded stones with occasional courses of Roman brick. The humming in my head intensified. I almost didn't hear it and I was forcefully drawn up the path to the front door. As with the Chapel of Bones, I knew that this too was part of the reason I needed to come to England. We pushed open the door and walked inside.

There was no one in the church. It was lit by a few rays of sunshine filtering through the trees outside and through the tall pointed gothic windows. A fat beeswax candle burned on each side of the altar. Their odor and that of a large arrangement of roses and white carnations underneath the lectern blended with the fragrance of the fading scent of incense. The walls were the same rough stone as the exterior, but had been covered with centuries of whitewash. Near the altar was a stone basin built into the wall. I knew that it was for pouring out the water used in the mass, but what was the name for it? I couldn't remember. Something to do with fish...pisces. That wasn't it, but something like that.

The ceiling was the underside of the roof, high and beamed with rough-hewn logs of massive size. Simple wooden benches faced the Cross hanging at the eastern end of the choir.

"I need to know more about this place," I commented as I looked around. "I mean, look at that basin near the altar, that pi, pice, oh what is it called? It certainly looks like it was added later than the wall it's in. I wonder if I could get into the archives of the cathedral, where they keep all the information about these little old churches. I'll write and ask."

Will didn't seem to hear me. He was looking around in wonderment.

"Wow," Will spoke very softly, "I think I could get religion in a place like this."

I sat down on one of the benches and Will followed suit. I stared at him. This was the man who had caused a big fuss with my parents by insisting that we be married by a justice of the peace because he didn't hold with this God stuff.

"Will," I said, "What do you mean when you say that?"

"What?" he was still peering up at the roof, a far-away look on his face.

"What you just said about getting religion, what does that mean?"

"Oh, I don't know, it's so quiet, so old, it feels like things have gone on here for... it was just something to say; what are you trying to get me to say? I didn't know you were so gung-ho about religion."

"Will, don't you see? When I'm in a place like this or other places that put me in touch with, with...I don't know, call it "the ages," I think that maybe time disappears and I could be here in other ages, that maybe I have been here in other ages. I feel as though I tap into something that takes me out of the everyday, something that is...oh, I can't explain it. But when you say you could get religion, I think maybe you're feeling something of what I am feeling."

"Yeah, well, I once heard a guy say that he could talk about his sex life a lot more easily than he could talk about his spiritual life. I don't know if I have a spiritual life, the very idea gives me the creeps, but I know I can't talk about it.

"Well I have a spiritual life. And I need to talk to you about it."

Will dragged his gaze from the beams in the ceiling and looked at me, warily. But he kept his response jocular. "OK, talk away." he said.

I took a deep breath. "I've never told anyone about this. Well, just one person. And I know it sound crazy, but I'm um...I'm psychic, Will. Clairvoyant."

Will squinted at me and his mouth opened. "You're what?" he asked.

"I see things, scenes, people from the past. And sometimes from the future. "

His face drained of color and I thought *Oh Lord, He's really upset by this.*

"Don't you think you might be imagining things?"

"I've been seeing these things all my life. When I was very little my mother used to say I was imagining things, too, and she would threaten to spank me if I spoke about it. But really, Will! I can see that you don't want to hear this stuff either, but I need to tell you. I used to see a woman in old-fashioned dress who was transparent. And she took care of me. At least she did most of the time."

Will continued to stare at me for several long seconds. He shook his head slowly. "Anything else?" he asked.

"Not if you don't want me to go on," I replied, my disappointment welling up with my tears.

"Marti, I'm sorry. I just can't deal with this right now," Will said. He turned and stood up, holding a pamphlet about St. Peter's up in front of him.

"Will," I shouted, "I wish you would say something. Talk about what you are feeling, please. "

"I can't," he said and he turned away, shaking his head. There was a moment's pause, and then, "Hey, isn't there supposed to be a leper's window or something here?" He looked around him.

I sighed as he helped me to my feet and we each began to skirt the walls. I walked along the west wall and Will along the north wall. We met at the corner where the walls came together and there, close to the floor, next to the small desk where some pamphlets and postcards were laid out, with an honor-system box for payment, was a hole in the wall about a foot wide and about eighteen inches high. The outer part had been screened and the inner was covered with cobweb-covered glass, crudely cut to fit the hole, and roughly mortared into place. The opening was very deep since the walls were about three feet thick at this level. By kneeling down, we could just make out the grass and part of a gravestone outside.

As I got down on my knees to look out the window, a familiar face looked in the window at me. "Oh, Will, look, there's Mr. Cooper peeking in at us." I pointed at the window and Will crouched down to look too.

"I don't see anybody, and why would he be looking in that little window instead of just coming in?"

We hopped up and ran outside, but saw no one.

"Marti, dammit, stop this. You're making me nuts, too."

Will started to walk toward the leper's window, his feet sinking slightly into the rain-softened earth. Suddenly he stopped. "Marti, your imagination really is working overtime again."

I looked up, about to protest, and saw what Will was pointing at. The earth under the tiny window was completely smooth. As Will walked, exaggeratedly pulling his feet out of the clay-like loam, he left large sloppy foot prints and his shoes were becoming caked with soil.

"Neither Cooper nor anyone else stood outside that window since the rain."

He sat down onto a horizontal gravestone and taking my two hands, pulled me down next to him.

"Marti, nobody looked through that window. If you saw Mr. Cooper, it was just in your head. Surely you see that?"

"Piscina!" I shouted.

Will looked at me as though he was sure I'd lost my mind.

"That's what that thing in the wall is called," I said sheepishly. "I couldn't think of the word."

He pulled me back against him, nuzzling the back of my head. "Well, life is not dull with you around, anyhow."

He looked around to see that there was no one to observe us and thrust his hand up under my shirt, cupping my breast as he kissed the back of my neck. *That's his solution for everything,* I thought. I stiffened momentarily then forced myself to relax and leaned back against him and sighed deeply. Would I ever get over that momentary fear of being hurt when Will started to make love to me? *It's not so bad*, I told myself.

"Listen," he murmured into my ear, "one night sleeping away from you has me having fantasies too. Let's get a room in an inn or a bed-and-breakfast tonight or better, still, let's find a haystack or a field or a hedge or something, I can't wait until tonight," He reached up under my brassiere with both hands and played with my nipples.

At the same moment Will and I both saw a huge old fir tree with branches that swept the ground like an immense skirt. A collection of upright gravestones surrounded the outer edge of its branches. I stared at it and felt myself becoming tense again. Will just turned to me and said, "Eureka!" Taking my hand, he pulled me up and led me to the tree. Underneath it was like a tiny room, enclosed by branches, perfectly dry, its floor soft with a carpet of dead needles.

Will sat on the ground and patted the dried needles next to him. I sat near him. I permitted him to unbutton my shirt and unfasten my brassiere. With soft pressure he pushed me down onto my back. He began to undo my jeans, nibbling at the same time at my bare chest, murmuring, "Oh God, how soft you are, like velvet." His hand under my buttocks, he lifted me, as he eased my jeans down over my hips, then pulled them down to my ankles. He started to tickle me, stroking my legs and inner thighs with feathery touches and stifling my giggles and little shrieks of "Will stop, don't..." with his mouth against mine.

When he was through, Will rolled over onto the soft floor and then stopped and put his hand under his back to extricate something that poked at him. He laughed. "Well, we're not the first to use this place," he said as he held up an empty condom package that had been partly buried in the needles. I lay there with my eyes almost closed. He looked at me lying very still, my face closed to him. Just then he noticed the injury on my knee and touched it gingerly. "How'd you get that?"

I didn't answer, slowly opened my eyes, and lifting my hips, began to pull up my jeans. Then I sat up and fastened my clothes. I looked at him without smiling and then put my head on my crossed arms supported by my knees. He wanted me to look more pleased with what had just happened, I knew, but I was startled as he began to speak of my reaction.

"You don't like this, do you?" Will looked very troubled. "Sex, I mean. You just sort of tolerate it. Look, Marti, I need to talk about this. I can't keep quiet about it any longer. I feel like I am doing something to you, rather than us doing something together. I just thought at first you were shy, that it was your proper southern aristocrat background, that you'd get to enjoy it more, but you're not.

Come on, Marti, say something, I can't do all the lovemaking and all the talking, too."

Will also sat up and rested his head on his crossed arms.

"Look," he looked up at me and his eyes were moist, his voice broke like a thirteen-year-old boy's as he spoke. "I know I'm not the last of the red hot lovers, but I want to please you. But how can I when you never speak? Almost never react at all. I might as well be making love to a, a potato!"

I raised my head and looked at him with astonishment. Seeing him on the verge of tears made me want to cry also, though not from a sense of injury, but from a more tender feeling for him than I had ever had before. I guess I just had assumed that Will's function in this marriage of ours was to take me to England and to protect me. And I would have to reward him for that service by letting him have sex. The idea that a man's role in sex had anything to do with giving his partner pleasure, rather than merely taking it for himself, was so alien that I had a hard time getting my mind around it. Yet I couldn't deny that I did feel pleasure at first when he caressed me. Just now I had felt lovely anticipatory tingles that had been overwhelmed, as usual, by my apprehension, my memories of previous injury and then my complete withdrawal into analytical detachment as I felt Will approach his climax.

"I'm sorry," I said softly, "I'll try not to be a potato, but I'm not sure I know how."

8
I Need Help 1349

BROTHER ANSELM, HIS legs quivering, stood holding on to the carved door of the chapel. He squinted through the smoky soot-filled air. Now that he had stopped, he became fully aware that his back muscles burned as though a coal were being held against them. He tried to take a deep breath, but could only pant.

The charcoal fires, in braziers at every turning of the monastery corridors, didn't cover the miasma of death that lingered in each corner, floated under the arched roofs and into the chapel. The light coming from the cloister and from the rounded windows in the north wall wasn't much help. Without the banks of candles at the altar, and at the feet of the statues of saints, he couldn't have seen at all.

Anselm hobbled to the font, feeling far older than his thirty years. He rubbed his hand across the stubble on his cheek. The water of the stoup reflected the candles' glow. As he bent over it, he could see his soot-darkened face as though in a mirror. He reached his finger into the holy water and dabbed it onto his forehead, his chest, and each of his shoulders, bowing to the statue of Christ above the altar.

He sank onto one of the stone seats lining the chapel wall, then turned and knelt, lifting his rough robe so he could feel the cool of the stone floor against the burning of the muscles in his legs. He rested his heavy head on his arms.

How long had he been carrying the bodies of the dead from the infirmary to the ossuary? He had brought the last body that morning and came back to the infirmary to find for the first time in ... it must be weeks... there were no newly dead bodies to remove. He had stopped counting the days since the first plague victim was found at the gate, burning with fever, his eyes yellow, his tongue black and protruding.

Since then, he had carried the bodies of his brother monks, one on each day, until it seemed as though the entire community would disappear. The Reverend Father had taken ill, his fever allowing him to see processions of angels walking through his room. But the fever subsided and he recovered, a sign, the brothers claimed, of Abbot Walter's sinless state. Even the Cathedral wasn't spared. Two Archbishops had died, one after the other. Anselm wondered what their sins had been.

Churches in the city were without priests. There was no one to offer the sacrament to the dying. Anselm had watched a constant stream of wagons, donkeys, and people with bundles on their heads, passing by St. Martin's gates. The healthy people fled to the countryside, leaving the ill to suffer and die untended.

But here at the monastery the discipline imposed by Abbot Walter was having its effect. It was amazing how they had managed to repair the roof, keep the infirmary clean and prepare wholesome meals for the sick. St. Martin's had become a hospice offering physical and spiritual care to the plague victims. Still, even here too many died.

Too tired even to pray, Anselm rested his head on the stone seat in front of him. Before the plague started, the new Abbot had been talking about tearing down these ancient crumbling stones and rebuilding in the new fashion, with huge windows pointing heavenward, branches rising to unbelievably high ceilings. Gloucester Cathedral had been rebuilt that way, and there were plans for such a new style in Canterbury Cathedral itself. Brother Anselm had seen the drawings the Abbot had commissioned and wondered where the money would be found to pay such skilled craftsmen. Now it was out of the question.

The last body he'd carried to the ossuary was that of the most prosperous farmer among the monastery's tenants, Hugh Attebrook. There'd be no rents paid to St. Martin's from that tenant, and so many like him, this year. Anselm recalled the dancing and feasting at the man's wedding two harvests since. The bride, Matilda, a child of thirteen, was so pregnant that she fairly waddled through the dancing, and had gotten stupidly drunk on nuptial beer.

He turned and looked up at the Christ on His cross over the altar. "Dear Lord," he whispered, "So few of us are left, so many dead bodies. How can those of us remaining do all the work that needs to be done?"

Anselm looked up at the painted ceiling as though the answers could be seen there. He began to rock back and forth. What if everyone died? Or if so many were gone that the rest could live only in savagery? Some even among his own brethren had committed terrible sins: no one knew that better than he. What sins had all the others committed, a sin so much worse than the usual human failings that God was punishing them so severely? He thought of Sodom and Gomorrah, of the Flood. "You promised you would not destroy all of us again," he spoke straight to the Lord.

Taking a deep breath and feeling some strength come back to him, Anselm pulled out his rosary and began his devotions. Suddenly a terrible memory from before the plague came into his mind. He was standing in the dark in an alcove on the stairs leading to the West Gate Tower. A figure carrying a large whimpering bundle was coming down the steps. He raised his hand as he had done that night. He would stop what was happening, he thought. Then he lowered it again just as he had done that night. He began to shake. A terrible sin had been committed and he had not prevented it, had not stopped it. He, of all people, should have done something. "Sweet Lord," he said, looking up again to the statue, "During all this time of illness, of death, of unspeakable terrors, of hell on earth, you have kept me well. With such a sin, how is it that I have not suffered punishment?"

The statue stared piercingly at him, a look both stern and very sad. Anselm felt an icy wind blowing from the altar. His body began shivering. It lasted but a moment and when it was over he knew, as though the knowledge had been chiseled into his brain, that his health was the punishment. He would not die, not now, not ever or possibly not until...

Tears began to run down Anselm's cheeks. "Thy will be done, Lord. As always." He bowed his head again until it rested on the stone seat. One candle began guttering, flaring up brightly before burning out. He looked up again at the statue, weeping his confession. "I have sinned Lord. You chose me because I knew what it was like. You gave me the opportunity to stop it and I failed you. I was weak and frightened. I didn't have enough faith." He whispered these words. "Oh God, I am so weak, so cowardly."

He held out his hands toward the statue. "I need help, Lord. You know that. You chose St. Augustine to preach your message to the people of Kent at St. Peter's church. But it was Queen Bertha who was your instrument to bring him there. You chose Moses to lead the people out of bondage. But you allowed him to call on his brother Aaron so that he would not have to meet that challenge alone." Then in a clear voice he declared, "I will try, dear Lord. With your help I will search for this person. I will make it come out right. But I need help."

9
The Cathedral Garden 1952

WE BEGAN THE long walk back through the old part of the city.

Will held my hand as we walked through the Butter Market and stopped to stare at the statues on the Christ Church Gate, the entrance to the Cathedral grounds. Each time I looked at him he seemed to want to say something. He would open his mouth, about to speak, and then shake his head slightly and stare ahead again. I wanted desperately for him to listen to me, to understand me, to accept me.

"Will," I finally began, my voice quavering, "you don't want me to talk about my psychic experiences, and I can't seem to talk about my sexual feelings as you would like me to. You're not sure whether you have any spiritual life, and I'm not even sure that I have any sexual feelings. How do we get around this?"

"It's not the same, Marti. You want to talk about stuff that's in your head, and I want to talk about stuff that's in your body."

"Oh, nonsense! It's all in our heads and in our bodies. You mean to tell me that you're not thinking anything, imagining anything, when you're making love? I don't believe it." To my surprise, Will blushed and then grinned.

We entered the Cathedral Precincts and found a little outdoor snack bar, where we got tea and sandwiches, taking them to a table far away from other people. A nearby shrub was turning a glowing crimson and was full of sparrows having furious debates.

"OK, Marti, here's what we'll do. I'll listen to whatever you want to tell me about your 'experiences' as you call them, if you would try to tell me what would really arouse you."

"Ha, ha," I said, "That's rich!" The mounting anger rose into my eyes so that I was seeing him through a red haze.

"Some deal! You'll 'listen'! What a sacrifice! I want to tell you something really important to me, and you'll deign to listen to me. I get to do all the work. What do you do? I didn't hear you promising to try to accept or understand what I am telling you. Or even to be open-minded about it. And I sure didn't hear you promising to share any of your feelings with me."

Will was bewildered and looked hurt, his brow furrowing up and his mouth beginning to droop.

"OK, try me. Tell me one experience. One that can't be explained by coincidence. And I'll try to be open-minded."

I sniffed and blew my nose. "All right. But I know you won't believe it. Last night I woke up and saw that the moon was shining in the window. Then suddenly a man floated in the window. He was a monk, but he looked like a younger version of Mr. Cooper. He took me by the hand and the next thing I knew I was in a medieval monastery, the one the Chapel of Bones belonged to, and I was carrying a heavy shovel and was all dirty, as though I had been digging graves. It was during the plague and I had been helping to bury bodies. At least that's what I assume I was doing. The shovel was too heavy for me and I fell down and scraped my knee. Then I realized that I had turned into a boy, sex organs and all. It didn't seem alarming, just sort of interesting. Then while I was in the latrine, peeing standing up, a monk came and tried to sexually molest me, and I pointed at him, and said 'Go away!' And the next thing I was in my sleeping bag in the youth hostel again."

"Marti!" Will rolled his eyes up at the sky and shook his head. He pushed the breadcrumbs on his plate into a ball and tossed it with great force overhand at some waiting sparrows. "I can't believe you are telling me this. It was a dream. A dream. D-R-E-A-M! You had a nightmare. Surely you don't believe that every time you dream, what happened in the dream was real?

"But I can prove it wasn't. When I woke up my knee was scraped and bleeding." I held up my injured knee. "Can you explain how that happened in a thick padded sleeping bag?"

"Maybe you were walking in your sleep and you fell down somewhere, or bumped into something."

"OK. Let me get this straight. You are suggesting that I unzipped my sleeping bag, climbed out of bed, went wandering around the hostel, fell or bumped into something hard enough to scrape a chunk of flesh off my knee, didn't wake up through all of that, climbed back into my sleeping bag and went on sleeping? I've never sleep-walked in my life. Why would I start now?" I was spitting my words out.

"Marti, there is a principle called 'Ockham's razor' which says that given any set of explanations, the simplest one is probably true."

"Yeah, yeah, I know all about it! But what makes your explanation any simpler than mine?"

"Because there are no ghosts. People do not float into windows. And people certainly don't go back in time and change sex."

"I am not crazy and I am not imagining things."

"Ok, this isn't getting anywhere. Let's call a truce about your experiences for the moment." He reached over and enfolded my hand to shake it. "Truce. OK?" I looked over my teacup at him and nodded warily. Will stroked my cheek. "I love you. Let's talk about making love. What is it that you would like me to do? To give you pleasure, I mean."

I quickly looked around to see that he could not be overheard. "Not here, Will." I whispered, "Someone might hear us."

"No one can hear us. And anyhow, who cares."

I looked straight ahead at the huge cathedral, shaking my head. I tried to calm myself by filling my vision with flying buttresses and towers. The autumn sunshine warmed the yellow-grey lichen-covered stones of the massive church, which seemed to glow with reflected light and with some internal energy of their own. Family groups in their Sunday best were forming and reforming for photographs, trying to get everyone into the picture while also getting in as much of the Cathedral as possible. "Shirley, a bit closer to Mum. Smile now Reg, there's a good lad."

I sighed. I was still irritated. But Will's hand still rested ever so tenderly on my cheek. He gazed at me so earnestly. I was torn about whether I could continue this discussion any longer. Will had asked me a monumentally ridiculous question in a place that only added to my feeling of exposure and vulnerability. I shook my head again. I was tempted to say, "I want you to leave me alone." But did I really? I had to admit that something was happening to me. Sex with Will was not awful. Maybe it was better than not awful. But how could I, sitting in a public place with people all around, drinking a cup of tea, try to imagine what I would like in the most intimate private times of my life? I wanted the whole subject to go away. I wanted the tug-of-war within me to drop. I sighed. "Okay." I said. I closed my eyes and tried to force myself to think about lovemaking. What would I like? I tried to imagine Will touching me, kissing my neck and my breasts. I began to feel a lovely warmth and smiled, closing my eyes dreamily. "Well," I began, "when you kiss my..." Suddenly a visceral shock, like a punch into my groin, caused me to catch my breath: The memory of being twelve, begging *him* to stop, as two powerful hands pulled my thighs apart and something hard and terrible was thrust into my body. The pain seared me, though I felt shiveringly cold, at the same time.

"Marti? When I kiss what? You started to say something. Can you tell me, I really want to know?" Will caught my hand. "Please, Marti, I really want to make you happy."

The tears welled up and my burning nose began to run. I scrubbed at my face with a handkerchief. An image of Anselm and of the Chapel of Bones came to me, summoning me. "Just leave me alone," I said as I wrenched my hand out of Will's.

10

I Shall Teach You 1952

I RAN AWAY from the Cathedral, leaving my husband open-mouthed.

"Marti, what did I do?" Will shouted after me, but I pretended not to hear him.

I pushed my way through the Sunday throngs that were pouring down the passageway into the Close. I ran down Mercery Lane. I burst out onto the High Street and began walking very quickly.

On the other side of the Westgate I hitched a ride with a middle-aged man in a bowler hat and high collar. When he stopped and pushed open the door of his ancient Morris Minor, he looked at me over his glasses and asked, "Just how far do you need to go, young woman?"

"Just about a mile or two," I tried to sound reassuring.

He obviously assumed that I was a much younger person. As the car chugged along at a stately speed, he lectured me about not accepting rides from strangers, "You are very lucky to be picked up by me and not some bloke with dishonorable intentions. What your parents would say, I hate to think."

I kept murmuring "Yes sir," and, "I'm sure you are right sir." But I bit my lips and clenched my fists to keep from screaming, "Go faster!"

As we came up the hill near to St. Martin's Lane, I suddenly said, "Oh this is it. Right here will do. Thank you."

The man looked surprised and a bit disappointed. "Are you sure this is where you want to go? Do you know someone on this lane?"

"Oh yes," I said, "the Coopers." Before he asked if my parents knew where I was, I thanked him again and bolted off down the lane. I had to get to the Chapel of Bones. I could be alone there and could try to think.

I walked very quickly. The sun had recently set and it was just dark enough so that I didn't think anyone on St. Martin's Lane had seen me come up from the High Road. The curtains were all drawn and no one look out as I passed by.

Out of breath, I sank down on a stone near the little building and listened first to the pulses beating in my temples, and then to the almost complete silence immediately around me. Far away a car down-shifted as it started up a hill and somewhere a bit closer I heard some music, as from a radio played at high volume behind closed windows. Close by some leaves fluttered to the ground and some small animal moved in the underbrush. I took a deep breath and closed my eyes. After a bit I was aware, without having heard anyone moving, that someone was standing near me. I kept my eyes closed and noted without surprise that I wasn't frightened by this, did not even feel the need to see who was there. I felt my right hand very gently being enfolded in a larger warm, strong one. I opened my eyes to see Anselm reach for my other hand. He pulled me to my feet. "Hi," I said, smiling at him. "Where are you taking me this time?"

He indicated the chapel with a turn of his head. In the next instant we were inside. Though it was completely black, I was able to clearly see the small circular bare room, and then two stools in the center. Anselm indicated that I should sit in one and he glided into the other

"You are not frightened?" Anselm leaned over and looked deeply into my eyes.

I shook my head. I was transfixed by the silvery grey of Anselm's eyes. They shone in the darkness like opals, with hidden depths of light and shadow.

"I summoned you, you know." Anselm said. "I need you. But first I need to know if you are truly the right one. Tell me how it is that you have this gift."

"Anselm," I said, "What could I possibly do for you? You aren't even alive, are you, though your hands are warm and I can't see through you. Sometimes I can actually see through people, you know, ghosts, I mean, not living people. Is that what you mean by my 'gift'?"

"Yes, yes, that's exactly what I mean. I don't know yet what it is that you can do. I think it will be revealed to us as we work together. As for whether I am alive or dead? Perhaps somewhere in between. I ceased to live, but I have not yet been allowed to have my rest. I have been wandering for six hundred years because there is something that I must do, but I don't know exactly how. And I must be helped by someone with your abilities." He took my hands again. "Speak to me about this gift. Who are the people who know that you can do these things? When were you first aware of it?"

"Well, I can see things and people from the past. Are you talking about that as well?"

Anselm nodded.

"Once in a while I can see the future, too. I've been trying to tell my husband about it, but he doesn't believe me. He thinks I'm crazy. And perhaps I am."

Anselm smiled. "Not crazy," he said very softly and shook his head.

"The only person I've ever told that I could see these things, besides Will I mean, is Mrs. Freedom. She's my family's housekeeper and she would sometimes see a woman behind her in a mirror who wasn't there otherwise, so she didn't think it strange when I told her about seeing the woman I called my 'see-through lady.' "

"Ah yes. Tell me about her."

In the old nursery the lamps had tea towels draped over them to keep the light dim and the shades were pulled down. I was five years old. Even in that low light I could see through the woman, truly through her, as though she were painted on the glass of the window. She stood looking at me from the right side of the pink canopied bed where I lay, sick with the measles.

As we looked at one another, the woman's face softened and she smiled at me as though we shared a secret. I smiled back. I could see the wallpaper on the opposite wall, the mantelpiece, even the doll's house placed on a low table so that I could arrange the furniture without getting down on the floor. All these things, I knew, should have been blocked from view by the woman's slender body, but I could see them with perfect clarity.

I lay absolutely flat on the bed, with a high fever. I didn't have a pillow. 103 degrees. My mother and Mrs. Freedom had taken turns sponging me with lukewarm water and now I had a cloth soaked with diluted rubbing alcohol and cologne spread over my itchy burning chest. My mother was sitting on the left side of the bed, reading Raggedy Ann aloud. It had been her favorite book.

I remember looking at my mother as though I were seeing her for the first time. Her hair, not one strand out of place, was smooth and rolled into a chignon on the back of her neck. I stared at my mother and I thought that her skin began to look like china and her eyes like blue marbles. As I looked into her eyes, I saw a tiny image of a woman in a nightgown, her hair all disheveled, sitting on the edge of a bed, weeping. My mother's voice retreated, becoming echo-like, hollow and ringing. She became blurry in the dim light. I reached out to touch her hand. It was quite cold.

I felt my own hair. Curly from the fever, it was a tangled mess all over the sheet beneath my head. How peculiar that my mother was turning to cold stone, while I was burning up! I looked back at the see-through woman who was watching me quizzically with one eyebrow raised. I tossed about the bed, tried to sit up and interrupted the reading with "Mama, who's that?"

"Shhh," her voice was distant, and she had to start over several times before it was steady enough to finish the sentence, "Stay still, stay, stay still, Martha. You'll get, get a headache sitting up. Who's what?"

As I started to say, "That lady in the long skirt," the woman put her right index finger to her lips and with her left hand patted my limp hand.

"There's no one there, Martha." The cold hand pushed me back onto the mattress. The words were spoken from a mouth that barely moved in a completely immobile face. "It's the fever making you see things. Now you must try to sleep."

"Mama," I whispered, so that my mother had to lean way over to hear me, returning as she did so to a flesh and blood person.

"Are there ghosts in this house?"

My mother fingered her pearls and adjusted her sweater on her shoulders. Her brows knit together. She looked beyond me for a moment. Then she reached down and patted my head. "You must stop listening to Mrs. Freedom, Martha. There are no such things as ghosts. It's just the fever," she repeated.

Taking a hard case from her sweater pocket, my mother removed her gold-rimmed glasses and snapped the case around them. She stood up briskly and pulled the covers up to my chin. "I'm going to give Mrs. Freedom a piece of my mind, going around frightening children. Now you just close those eyes and forget all about it." She bent over and brushed a kiss on the top of my head. I quickly raised my chin, trying to capture the kiss on my lips, but my mother moved away too quickly.

"I'm not frightened," I called after her and turned my head to see the woman again, just as she faded completely away.

"I've always been different," I told Anselm. "My mother was always trying to get me to be someone I was not: she always found things wrong with me. And she wouldn't protect me from... And my father..." I shook my head. I began to sob. As I said this, I could hear myself sounding like a small injured child. Anselm waited patiently as I cried, patting my hand. He pulled out a fine linen cloth from under his robes and handed it to me to wipe my eyes.

"Thank you." I sniffed and held the cloth.

"Did you see the lady again?"

"She saved my life. Or at least I would see her when I was in some danger, and then I would be saved. Although she didn't protect me from the worst things that ever happened to me."

Anselm nodded. "There are times when we need to save ourselves. But she is very important to you, Martha. I see that. And do you have any idea who this lady is?"

"Some sort of guardian angel, I suppose."

Anselm smiled. "Perhaps."

"Anselm, why can I see things from the past? And sometimes from the future? And why do I hear things? And you - why can I see you and speak with you? Am I the only one who can? What is it about me that makes me so different?"

Anselm put back his head and laughed heartily. He reached over, and patted my hand.

"You are delightful. Martha, come with me and I shall teach you. Your instincts are so good. You can see so much. Ah yes, you are definitely The One.

I started to ask him one what. What did he have in mind for me to do and where I was to go with him? Not back to the middle ages. That had been fascinating, but way too scary. Then I heard Will's voice outside calling my name.

"My husband. I have to go right now. He's probably going nuts with worry."

"Oh no, Martha." Anselm held on to my hand still. "You don't want to go to him, do you? Please. You must come with me. Here is an opportunity for you to help me right a terrible wrong."

I sat staring at the monk. I considered what he had said. Well, of course I wanted to go to Will! He was my husband. That is, at least I thought I did. Was Anselm saying that I had a choice? What was the choice? To go to be a boy in a medieval monastery? Not again.

Anyhow, there were things I needed to tell Will, things I needed to get him to understand. I was not ready to give up on my relationship with Will, nor for that matter on my life and my research. Though I had to admit I was intrigued by what Anselm had just said about teaching me. There were so many things I didn't understand about myself. What did he mean by saying I was the one?

"Ma-a-arti." Will's voice came closer.

"Yes, I think so. Yes that's what I want right now this minute." I gently detached my hand from his. "I will come again and we can talk about this some more. I need to know what you mean when you say that I am the one." I rose and walked toward the door. I found myself standing outside.

11
I Will Try 1952

THE CONFUSION AND emotional disarray that I had brought back to London with me from Canterbury had mostly been calmed by the week or two that I had been back at my research. I was very aware of having told Will that I would try not to be a potato. I had tried on a few occasions to start a sexual encounter, snuggling up against him or gently stroking the back of his neck. His response was so volatile that it frightened me - gunpowder on flames. My withdrawal from Will's passion would leave me curled up in my emotional hole once again, trying not to feel anything. Shrinking my mind away from Will's ardor, I would try to figure out what Anselm meant by saying I was "The One."

Now, however, I was back doing research, the place where I could really shine, glowing under the green library lampshade as though a spotlight radiated down on me. I held my hand with its bitten, raggedy-edged nails up to the light, imagining long painted fingernails and ovals of cuticles, smooth and round. I waved the hand slowly back and forth as though doing ballet until Will looked up at me with a puzzled look. I quickly put my fingers in my lap.

Sitting at a table in the main reading room of the British Museum Library, surrounded by stacks of books, I might be taking bows, though the audience could not be seen by anyone else. Two-story-high stacks of leather-bound volumes took up all sides of the room. The high ornate ceiling, the walls hung with balconied walkways, flat glass cases containing the Magna Carta, the Domesday Book, and other precious historic documents, the tables radiating out from the circular central catalogue, the hum of hushed voices; this was where I was meant to be. I was part of a parade of scholars down through the generations. As I sat there, I could see many of them, shadowy presences - mostly men, of course. I envisioned myself rising up and joining them, marching along in a stately file. I was only vaguely aware of what Darwin or Disraeli or Karl Marx or Marie Curie looked like, but I knew they were there. They didn't give me disapproving looks. I was simply one of them. Some day some other young woman would sit here and see Martha Davis Morton in this procession. I would be a great significant historian, someone who revealed how Roman survivals could be found in buildings from medieval times. My books would be on these shelves. And none of my admirers would fault me for unresponsive sex.

I leaned back in my chair and focused on the beautiful, high-domed room. How big was it, I wondered? Fifty feet by seventy-five, maybe? What if I started with the first book on the bottom shelf closest to the entrance and read my way all the way through the room, up and down, until I got back to the entrance again. How long would that take, I wondered? Probably several lifetimes.

If one just knew where to look, the answer to every imaginable question might be found here. I had a long yellow pad filled with questions for which I needed to find answers. The books I had requested were from some hidden place, far too mundane to be in these elegant precincts, brought in response to written forms filled with catalogue numbers and letters. Mostly I had been concentrating on Roman building techniques, and Saxon domestic architecture. In fact, the Saxon structures that had endured were made of reused Roman materials. They had often been made from the foundations of more elaborate buildings, abandoned and allowed to decay for scores of years after the Legions marched away. Now aerial photography had identified depressions and marks in the earth where Saxon villages had once stood, and

I was convinced that some of the ancient churches and other buildings had endured into the Dark Ages. I made lists of sites I wanted to visit. I mumbled Saxon words, names, and place names over to myself as I made notes: bretwalda, Mercia, Deira, Bernicia, Hengist, Oswy, Whitby, Aethelstan, burh. As I discovered and wrote down a Saxon word, others had come unbidden onto the page. At first I had looked up these unknown words to see if I had invented them. But every one was a real place or a real word. There was magic in them. I must have known theses words in some previous life!

I could just see Will's face over the small tower of books and papers in front of him, collections of judgments of manorial and ecclesiastical courts. He was looking in particular, I knew, for those which had attempted to prevent the wages of agricultural laborers from being raised in the aftermath of the plague. His concentration caused his forehead to crease and his lips to pull together as though by a drawstring. It made him look much older. He felt me gazing at him and looked back at me, his face relaxing into a grin so boyish that he suddenly looked about twelve. I had just a few minutes earlier wanted to punch him, but now I responded to his grin with a smile, only slightly less good-natured. I broke the gaze and looked back at my book.

We had just finished a hot argument in whispers about whether or not traces of the Roman laws and customs could be identified in the Saxon laws and customs and just which of these books would tell us. We had gotten into it because I was sure that when St. Augustine first got to Britain, St. Peter's had been a functioning British Christian church from the Roman era, while Will claimed that only in Ireland and Scotland and the west of England had Roman Christianity survived. Will insisted that the disintegration after the fall of the Empire and the barbarian invasions had forced the English communities to start from scratch, while I was sure that there had been a much greater degree of continuity. We had gotten distracted from our work by this dispute, which was silly and fruitless since we could, and undoubtedly would, pore through all of the books before us, and many others besides, to see which of us was right. But I was not going to let Will get away with any unfounded assertions. I had marshaled stacks of references on both Roman and Saxon communities in Britain. I had scribbled madly and hissed at Will, "Ha!" and "Wait 'til you see this," tapping my finger on the huge volume of Maitland.

We had arrived just after the Library opened and had now been working for almost two hours. That morning Will had stomped around the flat, quite unlike his usual cheerful self, glaring at me after another unsatisfactory attempt at love making. I had withdrawn so far into myself that I actually managed to fall asleep while he was trying to arouse me. I felt guilty about these encounters, but I knew that my withdrawal was how I had to protect myself. Now, as I pulled myself back from my daydream, I realized that I had read the same sentence over again for the third time and had still not registered what it said. I stood up. "Hey Will," I said, "Isn't time for "elevenses?"

We left our materials, telling the attendant that we would be back in a few minutes, and went to the Library lunchroom for some coffee.

Will pushed away his raisin cake, sat looking at me and now shook his head. He looked around to see that no one was close enough to hear him and then spoke in a low voice anyway, his face close to mine. "I don't understand you. You can be so tough and assertive and sure of yourself when it comes to your field. Or almost anything. It was one of the things that attracted me to you in the first place, the fact that you seemed like such an independent woman, not at all a clinging vine."

"Well I am." I looked at him with a pugnacious expression, chin thrust out. I tried to push my guilt away with an attitude of toughness. "So what is it that you don't understand?"

"How can someone so well-put-together be such a passive creature about sex? In every way but that you are so much more advanced than any other woman I've ever known, but where sex is concerned you are shy and prudish and ignorant. You just lie there. It's as though your mind leaves town and an inanimate body gets left behind. You act like you don't feel anything? Don't you want to feel anything?"

I felt my cheeks coloring and I looked down at my hands. Hunching over and talking to my knees, I spat out, "You do find the most peculiar places to discuss this subject. Cathedrals and museums. Maybe you'd like to hire a billboard in Leicester Square."

"Don't be ridiculous! No one else can hear me. You're just avoiding the subject. What happened to you? I keep wondering what you were taught about sex? Anything?"

I looked long and hard at Will from under lowered brows, my face stony, not revealing the panic I felt. Yes I had been taught about sex, alright. My father had taught me that I was a thing, a powerless victim. And my mother had taught me, though never in so many words, that I had better never talk about it.

My mother must have heard my father come into my room. Sounds carried clearly in my family's old house. But she couldn't have cared, because the next morning she acted as though nothing had happened. Now I knew that if Will kept at me about this I would have to stop avoiding what had been done to me and might even have to speak about it. *Get ahold of yourself,* I heard my mind saying. Then I sat up straight and stuck my chin out again. "I learned the anatomical details in a health class in junior high, and before that from some dirty little cousins who kept trying to pull my panties down, until I kicked one of them in the groin with my little Maryjanes. Which ought to be a warning to you!" I continued in a less belligerent tone. "My mother never taught me anything that anyone would want to know. But I guess I learned, without anyone ever talking about it, that I needed to lie still and submit. It's very hard to unlearn. But Jesus, Will, why is it so God-damned important? You seem never to think of anything else. I don't keep you from having sex whenever you feel like it. Why do we keep having to discuss it?"

"Submit! Yeah that's exactly what you do, submit. Like it is something nasty and disgusting that you just have to get through. A dose of castor oil. How do you think that makes me feel? It sure doesn't do anything to make me feel appealing or sexy." Will's nose turned red and his eyes looked wet.

I reached my hand to his and held it silently for a moment. "Sugar, we have so much fun together in so many other ways. Is this really so important?"

"You're damned right it's important. It is the most important thing in any marriage."

"Oh, come on!" I said, blowing my breath out contemptuously, "Men always think that sex is the most important part of marriage. Maybe it is for them."

"Aw, don't give me that. Sex is or can be one of the greatest pleasures in life. For men AND women. When it isn't, there is something wrong. Sure, I know it can be awful. I know that it has to be good for both, otherwise it is torture, rape, abuse. But when it is, it is a - a - a gift. That's what it is, a gift, and I want us to give it to each other."

"Thank you Dr. Kinsey. Now can we go back to our work?"

I began to gather up our coffee things to take to the scullery. Will blew out his breath and clucked his tongue against the roof of his mouth. But he reached out and held my shoulder, keeping me in my seat. "Marti, will you let me try to show you how wonderful it can be? You said you would try to overcome this? Please?"

"Will, I've really been trying, but I don't even know how to begin."

"Let me begin, OK? Marti, will you trust me?"

I looked at Will for a long time, neither of us saying anything. I tried to see deep enough into his eyes, as though some magic signal light or reassuring image would shine out for me. But all I saw were warm brown irises and long black lashes, contrasting with his blondish hair. The question kept beating in my brain: who are you?

He really was such a nice guy that I had let myself believe he understood. But it turned out that he was still a guy, superior, condescending at times, pig-headed, and from my point of view, obsessed with sex. And he rejected my mystical ability, surely the most important part of me. Until I could convince him of my gift of knowing things, I couldn't really trust him completely in other essential ways. Or could I? Could I look at sex as a gift we gave each other, instead of something Will was seizing from me, when he couldn't accept the most important gift I had to offer? On the other hand, maybe, just maybe, if I could seem more responsive, he'd be more open about what was vital for me. I couldn't hope to enjoy what other women did when it came to sex, but perhaps I could at least try to get past what had been done to me.

I sighed. I looked at Will for a long time, neither of us saying anything.

"I would like to. But I don't know if I can. Not yet anyway. But I will try, I really will try."

12
The Lesson 1952

I FED SIX big copper pennies into the coin slot of the "geyser", the hot water heater in the bathroom we shared with the other three bed-sitting flats in the basement of the Victorian house in Clapham South. Unless one followed some other bather immediately, the room was as cold as the unheated hallway. Since I liked to soak and luxuriate for about forty-five minutes, until the water began to cool, I generally bathed in the afternoon when none of our neighbors were around. Through shivering trial and error, I had determined that a sixpence-worth of hot water was exactly the right amount to fill the tub just enough so that it didn't overflow when I got in. It also steamed up the room sufficiently to take the chill out of the air. The tub in the bathroom was about half-again as long and possibly twice as deep as a standard American one.

In college in New York I had jumped in and out of the shower every morning for no more than five minutes, but bathing in London was such a lengthy production that I only allowed myself the indulgence a few times a week.

As the steam billowed around me, I unbraided my hair and brushed it one hundred strokes. I placed my big thick towel on the heated rack next to the tub, and my flannel bathrobe beside it, both close enough to grab as soon as I climbed out of the tub. I poured lavender bath salts under the hot tap and inhaled deeply.

I lowered myself slowly into the almost scalding water, allowing each part of my body to gradually get accustomed to the heat. I leaned back so that the water came up to my chin and I had to hold on to the side of the tub to keep from floating away. I lathered each leg in turn, flexed, stretched and then rinsed it off. I washed each part of me slowly, making a satiny sudsy frosting on my arms, my breasts, my groin, between my toes.

I leaned way back to allow the water to rise around my face until just my eyes and nose were still exposed. My hair floated on the surface like a copper cloud.

When the water had cooled to only slightly warmer than the air, I arose and preened before the steam-fogged mirror on the back of the door, imagining myself Botticelli's Venus. I rubbed myself vigorously with the towel, then wrapped it around my hair like a turban. I rubbed lotion caressingly over all of my skin before snuggling into the warmed robe.

Emerging from the warm room, I floated across the cold hall to the flat, which we kept at a higher temperature than most English people would tolerate. The gas fire under the mantelpiece in the main room took shilling pieces to keep it going. Two overstuffed chairs with threadbare pink linen slipcovers sat facing each other on either side of the fireplace. We had removed the crocheted doilies from the backs and arms of the chairs, and had bought standing lamps to put behind each one, to supplement the glaring 50-watt bulb in the middle of the ceiling. The beige conical shades bathed each of us in a circle of soft yellow light, and I had found two bright orange knitted throws in a second-hand shop to snuggle in while we read. We covered the wallpaper, which had hideous huge brown cabbage roses, as much as possible with travel posters begged from airline offices on the Haymarket. A rickety gate-leg table and two cane-seat chairs, an ornate chest of drawers, its veneer peeling in places, and a four-poster double bed completed the furnishing of the room. To combat the basement dampness and the smell of the gas heater, I kept a bowl of rose petals and oranges studded with cloves in the middle of the table.

We usually kept the radio tuned low to the BBC Third Programme. Bursting into this combination bedroom, living room, and dining room, I heard Mozart's Eine Kleine Nachtmusick softly playing and found Will lying on his side on the bed, naked.

"Hi," he said, "care to join me?" He held out both arms toward me, with his palms upward. His mischievous grin revealed how delighted he was with himself.

I could feel myself turn red. "For God's sake, Will, you haven't even pulled down the shades." I had seen Will without clothes, of course, but it still made my skin get all goose-bumpy to look openly at his genitals, now lying flaccidly along one long thigh. I fussed with pulling down the window-shade and closing the cheap lace curtains, though I knew perfectly well that the interior of our flat could only be viewed by someone deliberately kneeling down on the grass of the small ornamental back garden.

Will patted the comforter next to him. "Stop fooling with the window, Marti and take that robe off. We're going to have a sex lesson."

"But it's the middle of the afternoon!"

"So?"

"But... this is a nutty time, what if someone... um, what if... " I strained to think of some good reason, beside the fact that it was an unconventional time for us to be together undressed, and then what Will had just said sank in.

"What do you mean 'a sex lesson'"?

Will raised himself on one elbow. "Look, Martha Elizabeth Davis Morton, you are a very smart woman. And, without question, you are the most beautiful woman I know. But when it comes to love-making we both know... Well, let's just say it is too one-sided." He blew air from between his lips as though he had been running. "I'm tired of doing all the work." He was still smiling at me, but a wistful quality had entered. Now I stared directly at his pale body which seemed to gleam against the brown plaid of the comforter.

I could hear some bird singing liquid trills and gurgles in the shrub outside the window. I looked down and fingered the stitching on my robe's sash. I started to protest, "Will, I can't. I'm no good at this sort of thing." But he cut me off, lifting his head even further from the pillow to look right into my eyes. "Marti, I love you. We agreed that this has got to be good for both of us. Come on. What do you have to lose?"

I shook my head. I didn't know exactly what I had to lose, but I felt as though it wasn't just my skin that was being exposed.

Usually when we had sex, Will removed my clothes from my limp unmoving form. In fact Will did everything. He stopped to gaze at my body in the process, to stroke me and kiss each part as he uncovered it. And although I usually could feel my skin begin to tingle, I kept my eyes tight shut, as though that fended off my vulnerability.

Now, however, I bit my lips, sighed deeply and nodded. I untied the sash and rubbed it against my cheek. I took off my robe, carefully folding it and placing it over the back of a chair. My muscles, which had almost melted in the bath, were now so tensed up they might twang. "What do you want me to d-d-do?" I said. My teeth began chattering and I knew it was not the temperature.

"Marti, I'm going to make a few suggestions to get you started. But you take the lead this time. Who knows? Maybe you'll get inspired. Now sit here on the bed where we can touch each other."

"I'm...I...I don't think I can do this, Will." I stood there hugging my chest. I was tempted to put one hand over my pubis like a renaissance nude, and giggled at the thought or maybe it was just from nervousness.

"Marti, come on. Sit here." He patted the comforter.

I sat. I looked solemnly at Will's face. He grinned at me and blew a kiss. "Smile," he said. I smiled nervously. He took both of my hands. "C'mere," he said, pulling me over so that my upper body was in contact with his chest, my head resting on one of his shoulders. I inhaled the toasty scent of his skin. He then lifted my lower body so that my legs were astride his thighs. "Now could you maybe kiss me?" It sounded more like a plea than a demand. I lifted myself so that my lips could reach his, and found his open mouth waiting for me. Starting with my lips closed, I pressed them onto his, then found my body relaxing, my mouth opening.

Uncertainly, I darted my tongue into his mouth. Very tentatively I began to move my tongue around, first rubbing it on the insides of his lips, then venturing more boldly further into his mouth, finally encountering his tongue. Suddenly I was aware of the pressing on my lower abdomen of his hardening penis, and I drew in my breath and sat up, my arms hugging my chest.

"Something wrong?" Will whispered.

"I don't know what you want me to do next," I said.

"Whatever you'd like to do, but please don't stop."

"But what would you like?"

"Ha!" he said. "That's my line. You could just keep kissing me, but now how about working your way down my body, a little at a time."

I kissed his eyes, his cheeks, his chin, his neck with delicate little caresses. I giggled again. This was beginning to be fun. When I got to his chest, I can't imagine what possessed me to take one of his nipples between my lips and lick it. Will moaned. "Oh, I'm sorry," I sat up quickly, "did I hurt you?" Will's answer was to pull me down to his chest again, and whisper, "Do the other one please, just the same way."

As I proceeded, Will lay with his arms at his sides, his legs apart, and a delighted grin on his face. Now as I worked my way down to his navel, he laughed out loud. "Hey, babe, you're great! My star pupil!"

I rested my face on his abdomen, asked, "How many other pupils have you taught?" I didn't expect him to claim innocence, but I felt a pang of... could it be jealousy?... when he said, "Not more than twenty or so."

"You're kidding, right?" Twenty? "That's ridiculous!"

Now I was face to face with his erection and I could not go on. I rolled off him and lay down next to him, reaching over to pull the loose edge of the comforter over me. "Ok, I'm through!" I said breathlessly, and realized that my heart was pounding.

"What do you mean 'you're through?' You've just gotten to the best part. You can't stop now!"

"You want me to kiss that?" My voice became more high-pitched as I pointed in the general direction of his groin.

"Why not? Isn't it as lovable as the rest of me?" Will chuckled. "Look babe, you don't have to do anything that you feel squeamish about. Just consider the fact that oral sex may be as good a way of enjoying yourself as any other." His voice lowered. "And it sure would give me a great deal of pleasure."

"No, Will. I couldn't. Please don't ask me to."

"OK, but here is this perfectly good erection going to waste. What are you going to do about that?"

"What should I do?"

"How about getting on top of me and maybe something will occur."

"You mean having sex with me on top?"

He took my hand and kissed each of my knuckles.

"Could you do that?" he asked.

The very last rays of the almost horizontal sun came through the window, shining right onto the bed where we lay. The bird outside the window stopped singing and the whole flat seemed to fill with an expectant silence.

I pulled myself up onto him again. With me on top I felt in control. I took him into me, amazed at how effortless it seemed. It was a glorious feeling. I almost wanted to shout. I made a few tentative motions of my pelvis that felt tantalizingly good. I began to move myself up and down, slowly at first, then faster and more vigorously until all at once a delicious explosion occurred inside of me and I collapsed panting onto Will.

"Oh my God," I whispered, "I think I had an orgasm!" Right on cue the bird started up again.

"Hooray!" Will shouted and by thrusting his whole torso, bounced both of us up and down. He threw his arms around me and kissed me passionately. I burst into tears.

"Christ! Now what?" Will went from joy to dismay in an instant. I began to sob uncontrollably.

"Marti, shhh. Don't cry. It's alright. You were great. I love you," he babbled as my hot tears coursed down his chest.

I could not speak for several minutes, my breathing ragged. Finally my voice came out, rasping and almost incomprehensible. "I was raped. Will. I was raped. Raped! That's why it is so hard. I've been so frightened and..." I began to cry again quite hysterically, unable to stop as sobs racked my whole body.

Will just held me and over and over whispered, "Shh." He kissed the top of my head and patted my back. I could feel the iron tightness of his jaw, but his touch was gentle.

13
Afterwards 1952

ALL THESE MANY years I had kept that horrible memory at bay. Each time the vision of being pushed down on my bed, hearing myself whimpering, "No, Daddy. Please, no," would overtake me, I would force myself to think about something else. I would open my book and enter the pictures of the medieval places. I would plot revenge and getting away.

But that London winter afternoon, as the early darkness crept through the window, I lay curled under my old plaid comforter, weeping. Even though Will held me in his arms, the empty, violated feeling replayed in all its vivid detail. It wasn't the love-making that brought it all back. Will had managed to overcome my resistance to sex early in the weeks since our wedding, without my being much more than unresponsive. It had become a game. He would initiate. I would resist or feign indifference. Mentally and even sensually I would retreat into some other place. After a while I even began to like it, sort of. I liked the tenderness of his caresses. I giggled nervously, but I had to admit that I was pleased by his unreserved enthusiasm for my body. I found myself looking forward to the warmth I felt when he embraced me. I even enjoyed the faintly musky smell of his skin combined with soap and shaving cream. But now that I had experienced that glorious love-making, I felt in terrible danger. I had given Will a fragile, vulnerable part of myself. I had revealed my secret.

I felt as though I were walking across a glacier with crevasses opening at my feet. Under Will's tutelage I had come to that sublime and terrifying climax. But he had gotten under my defenses and I had broken down and told him.

That day Will held me until I sobbed myself to sleep. I slept as though in a coma, hardly moving most of the time, and not responding when he put his lips to my forehead and whispered, "Marti, do you have a fever?" Occasionally during that long evening and night I was partly aware of shuddering and whimpering in my sleep, and of Will patting and stroking me each time.

The next day, when I awoke, I commented on the fact that it was raining again. I wondered aloud if it might snow, the clouds had that snow-filled look. I nibbled on the toast that Will made for me. I mentioned that we needed to take the laundry out.

Will cleared his throat. "Marti." He spoke very softly. "About yesterday..."

I rode over his beginning with, "Will, make sure you put the towels into the bag."

"Marti," he began again a little more loudly. "Please talk to me. I'm your husband. I love you. Please, I need to know - who, when, where - what happened?" He reached out and took my arm, forcing me to look at him.

I looked blankly at him and then away again. I just sat there looking at the tweed place-mats my college roommate Carol and her husband Freddy had given us. Out the window I could see the last leaves twirling down from plane tree at the bottom of the garden. I pushed his hand away. I turned my back on him and shook my head.

I turned pages in my book, stopping to stare long and hard at the page with the little ossuary peeking out from behind the monastery buildings, the long line of monks walking toward it in my mind's eye.

Will kept trying. He reached out and lifted my chin with one gentle finger turning my face back toward him. "Marti, something terrible happened to you, and you've got to talk to me about it. Everything was going so wonderfully. You've got to tell me who it was that did that to you."

I turned another page in my book and then, without looking at him, asked, "Is there any coffee left?" Will poured me some and waited for me to say something. I sat very still for a long while, sipping my coffee. Then I stood up. "I've got to go to the library," I said. He just sat there open-mouthed as I walked out the door.

Weeks went by and I adamantly refused to speak to Will about anything more consequential than "pass the salt." I threw myself into my studies with manic energy. Each night I curled in my big chair, under the single reading light. The rest of the flat was hidden in shadows. I refused to come to bed until long after Will was asleep, creeping out again before he awoke. I treated him as though we were two barely-acquainted roommates. I remained courteous and calm. But I spent as much time as possible in the library. And I waited for the explosion I expected would come from him. And I decided that when he exploded, I would walk out on him.

Will and I had different schedules, mine governed by course times; he was mostly at the British Library. Going to and from the University, I sat in the train listening to the roar and staring at the walls of the Underground tunnel flying by. I began to see images from the last time I had been with Anselm. I remembered his gentle concern. He was so easy to talk to. He was going to teach me something. Something about myself, about my gift. The scene with him inside the little chapel replayed in my mind, driving away the terrible memories of the rape, and the equally terrible dilemma of whether I could bear to stay married. I began to feel with increasing urgency that I needed to see Anselm again.

One evening, as usual, I sat up trying to read in front of the gas fire, snuggled in the old armchair with its frayed pink slipcover. I couldn't concentrate, however. I kept changing position and was preoccupied with how I would find Anselm if I did go back to Canterbury. I looked up from my book to find Will looking fixedly at me from the bed.

"I thought you were asleep, " I said.

Will shook his head and continued to look at me.

"What's the matter; can't sleep?" It was the first time in several weeks that I had asked him anything besides questions about the weather.

Will raised himself up on one arm and said, "Marti, we can't go on like this. Why are you freezing me out?"

I looked at the ugly stained wallpaper above Will's head. I didn't answer and I could feel my lips shriveling into a tight line.

"Marti, did I do something terrible without realizing it?"

That made me look directly at him, startled. "You? No, of course not. It isn't you. Well, not exactly. It's me."

Now he sat all the way up. "What does that mean 'not exactly'? What is happening? Marti, please talk to me."

"Will, I need to work this out for myself. Please be patient with me."

"Marti, what are you working out? If I'm not the problem then why can't I help?"

"Look, I don't expect you to understand this. I have to go back to Canterbury to find out something. To see someone who can help me figure it out."

"Canterbury? What can you possibly find out in Canterbury? And who's there who can help you?" I could feel my face go stony again. "You're right. I don't understand it at all. How about trying to explain it to me? Don't you think you owe me that much?"

I shook my head. "I've just got to go there."

"OK, then I'm going with you."

"No. I don't want you to. I've got to do this by myself."

Will threw himself out of bed and stood glaring down at me for several minutes. The gas fire popped in the silence. He pointed his finger at me as he spoke. "OK, do it by yourself, but I just might not be here when you get back."

My face burned as my temper, dormant these many weeks, flared. "Don't threaten me, Will. I just might not come back."

14
We Can Help Each Other 1952

THERE WAS A cold wind blowing and a few drops of rain fell as I walked up St. Martin's Lane and into the woods surrounding the Chapel of Bones. The clouds were racing furiously across the sky, occasionally allowing a few rays of sun to appear. The rhododendron leaves were shriveled into tightly curled tubes and all the other trees were bare. The dried, dead leaves formed a crunchy frozen carpet underfoot.

As the chapel came into view I saw someone kneeling on the icy ground. My heart rate increased. He hopped up, then kneeled again, repeating this several times. Now once again, he fell to his knees on the frozen earth. When he stood, I could see the monk's robe with hood pulled up so that his face was hidden. I knew, however, that it was Anselm.

I stood still watching. He was so absorbed in rising and kneeling again, pausing to say his beads, mumbling something to himself, that he seemed to have lost all awareness of his surroundings.

"Why do you keep hopping up and down?" I spoke softly, but it startled him so that he bolted upright and the hood fell back. He looked as though he could not believe his eyes. "Martha," his voice broke and he swallowed several times, "you have come. I have been praying and praying for you to come back."

"Anselm, aren't you cold? You are wearing only your woolen robe. Or don't ghosts get cold?"

I was shivering, despite a heavy wool coat with a zip-in fur lining and long underwear beneath my jeans.

"Can we go into the Chapel?" I turned to Anselm and asked. "At least it's out of the wind in there. I need to talk to you." Suddenly the knapsack I was carrying on my back felt encumbering. I shoved it into a shrub near the Chapel door.

A thin stream of sunlight filtered through one of the narrow windows, hardly warming the centuries-old chill. Sitting again on the two stools, we looked hard at one another. We spoke simultaneously. "I need your help," each of us said and then stopped. I laughed and Anselm smiled at me.

"Then," Anselm took my arms below the elbows, "you must tell me how I can help you, and I will tell you what you must to do to help me. We can help one another."

"Well, all right, you see I was... no, you go first. I'm not ready to speak about this yet."

"I must tell you about the sins that were committed, the acts of courage that were omitted. You must know my story so that you can help me to make right.

"As you know, I was a member of the Benedictine order, and I lived all my life from infancy in the Abbey of St. Martin's, here in Canterbury." His voice became like a chant, blending into the hum I heard as I looked around at the embedded bones. I had difficulty concentrating on what he was saying.

"I was cared for by my dear brother and foster-father, Brother David. He taught me to be a monk. He taught me the lives of the saints and how they suffered for our Lord's sake so that they would be an example to me. Except that I chose the one, St. Augustine of Kent, whom I have always revered for his quiet, ordinary competence, who did not suffer, but still served the Lord. I was so fearful of the prospect of the suffering, you see, that I attached myself to Augustine. When David died I became the Abbey's chronicler in his place."

Augustine, again Augustine. It made me think of Will.

"My choosing Augustine is significant, I see now. I was myself chosen by Augustine also, since he gave me a treasure, his journal."

"His journal?" He had my whole attention. "St. Augustine had a journal?"

"Yes. He kept a journal. That is what I have been telling you."

I had been growing more and more puzzled, trying to hear what might involve me in this recounting of Anselm's life and why the saint's name resonated. Now my mouth opened with surprise and I whispered, "Wow, no kidding!"

Anselm smiled and nodded his head, holding my arms even more firmly. "Now, however, I believe that I was chosen in a different way. You see I did suffer, horribly, but I was so young at the time I could only think, as I had been taught, that if I suffered it was as a punishment for my sins. But that was not my sin. I was chosen because of my own suffering to help others in the same peril, the boys who were mistreated, but I turned away. I must go back to live it all over again, but this time I must stop the evil. "

Anselm's grey eyes seemed to glow with an inner fire and I could not stop staring into them. They grew larger and larger and I saw far down into them an image of a small naked boy being held face down on a cot and a man on all fours above him. I shivered and gave a long shuddering sob. Anselm closed his eyes. "You see that! Oh, of course you can see into my soul. Oh, merciful Lord. You must not look," he said breathlessly, hardly moving his lips. I saw tears emerging from under his lashes. With my tears beginning to fall onto my cheeks as well, the bond between us was powerfully obvious to me.

"Anselm!' My voice rose excitedly. "Now I understood why we had been drawn together. Look at me! It was the same for me. Truly! Not the saint stuff. But the rape. The betrayal. The ones who should have been caring for me, protecting me, loving me, were the ones who violated me. My father raped me and my mother pretended that she didn't know. You and me, we each were robbed of a part of ourselves."

I grabbed his arms now as he opened his eyes once again. "Don't you see? Oh, I see now. I've always assumed that no man could understand. That everyone would think it was my fault, that if I ever had a husband he would be repelled by me if he knew. But you can understand. Maybe if we can tell each other the things we've never told anyone, we can each begin to, to... "

Anselm shook his head. "Telling is not enough. I need you to really help me."

"What can I do?"

"Martha," he drew in his breath several times, to inflate his courage, "Come back with me to that time. You will not be Martha, but a novice, Martin, whose patron saint is the same as the abbey's. You will be, you are, one of the boys who were stolen, and I will be your rescuer. This is the only way for it to end. I know this. Please say you will do this."

I laughed, "Oh sure," I said, "And then will we go to Cambridge, Maryland so you can keep my father from getting into my bed?"

Anselm jumped back as though I had struck him and looked at me. His mouth fell open and his eyes grew wide. "Ah, you think, quite rightly, that I am only thinking of myself. You also have a terrible wrong that needs to be put right. But Martha, that is outside my power."

"But Anselm, why?"

Anselm shook his head. "It is not in my power," he said again. "It is for you, yourself, to make that right. But that can happen if you come with me."

I went completely still. I never doubted for a moment that it was possible for me to go with him. I could feel a numbing fear penetrating me like the cold. I could only take quick, shallow breaths. That last time in the youth hostel it had been scary, but fascinating, like a strange dream, not quite real. What if I couldn't get back and I had to remain in the 14th century? I stood up and began to pace around the walls of the chapel, stirring up the dust that swirled in and out of the beam of window light. I reached out one finger to touch the bones embedded in the wall. I felt a shock of vibration and a burst of humming.

"Why me?" I asked Anselm. "And why now? Why not get a boy and take him back and rescue him? Surely I'm not the only person you've met in 600 years who has the 'gift' as you called it. And how do you know it will work?"

"All this time I have been looking for the one person. The right person. You saw into my soul and saw what happened to me. I am certain as I never have been before that you are that one.

"Now here is what we must do."

I kept shaking my head as I listened to Anselm's plan. I felt my insides dissolving in terror, and at the same time a tantalizing curiosity. The very idea was absurd, unreal, but I could feel myself being pulled.

"Look Anselm, I'd like to help you, but I don't see how any of this will help me." I held my hands out in front of me, as though weighing the pros and cons. I looked into my right hand and mumbled to myself. "It would be amazing to see the medieval period first hand…" I looked into my left hand a spoke a bit more clearly, "But how do I know I won't get stuck back there and not be able to come back to the present?" I shook my left hand. "And how would someone who grew up in the 20th century know how to behave, how to speak, in the 14th century? I mean, I'm a woman! What do I know about how little boys act? I never even had any brothers. I probably won't understand anything people say to me. And how do I know you will rescue me? What if I get raped again! No, I can't. I just can't."

"Martha, you must trust me. Else why did you come here? Why did you seek me out again? I will protect you."

I shook my head. I walked back and forth in front of Anselm. I began to cry as I remembered Will saying, "I just might not be here when you come back." Was my telling him that I might not come back a presentiment, or just idle words said in anger? Had I already burned my bridges?

Anselm watched me. "Why do you weep, Martha?" he said gently. He stood and took my hands. "What is it that you want?"

"Want? I want these horrible memories, these paralyzing fears to stop. I want to feel free, free of the guilt. I want to be able to make love with my husband and feel joy. I want to do really important work, to get recognition as an historian, to make some discovery, find out something that no one else has ever known before.

"I would like to help you, Anselm, I really would. But you ask too much. I can see why you think I might be the one who can help you. When you tested me that last time, (it was a test wasn't it,) and I handled being in the 14th century pretty well, you figured that I could do this for you. If I came back to the twentieth century and tried to tell anyone, no one would believe me, they'd think I was making it up, or hallucinating. Would it make me more fearless, more able to make love, a better historian?"

Very faintly, so soft that I might have been imagining it, I thought I heard a choir.

"Martha, I can give you something that would prove that you have done something remarkable. Remember I told you that the Blessed Augustine had given me his journals?" I nodded, wiping away my tears. "Well, I have hidden them at St. Peter's. If I told you where to find them, what would you be able to do with them?"

I gazed at the chapel's walls. Some of the bones seemed to glow.

I started mumbling to myself: "Some way of authenticating them… Probably have to determine the age of the vellum and the composition of the inks… Someone who can read sixth century Latin… Or I'd have to learn…" I noticed the tiles on the floor of the chapel. There was something familiar about the pattern in which they'd been laid. They too began to glow and very faintly take on color. I gave a long exhalation. Still staring at the pattern on the floor, I reached for Anselm's hand.

15
The Novice 1348

REDS, BLUES, YELLOWS, and greens lay on the floor in patterns from the stained-glass rose window above the altar. I felt a sharp blow to the side of my head. I was again in a strange place, another time, standing among a double line of young boys in the raised part of the nave of a chapel. Banks of candles lit our faces; across the aisle, rows of brown-robed adult monks were similarly illumined. From the horizontal rays of sunlight filtering down through the candle smoke I guessed that it was late afternoon. But inside the chapel, darkness hovered in the corners not touched by these lights. An old monk was glaring at me, brandishing the long rod with which he had just struck me. I put my hand to the smarting place on my ear, and opened my mouth to protest. "Pay attention, Martin," he hissed in a loud whisper. "You will never learn your part if you gather wool in that way. And put your hand down, clasp the other one, like this. Now sing out... 'summo Christo decus, Spiritui Sancto.'"

The boys on either side of me grinned from within their cowls and nudged one another, moving almost imperceptibly away from me. I understood the old man perfectly, despite the fact that he sounded like a character out of Chaucer. Once again I was wearing a woolen tunic of itchy, grey homespun fabric and baggy, woolen hose, but this time the garments were relatively clean. I had not been digging graves in these clothes. A black hood covered my head and soft leather shoes were held on my feet with knee-high laces.

I realized I was on my own here. "I don't even know the song," I murmured under my breath and then was amazed as I heard myself singing out the Latin words with some fluency and an obvious knowledge of the music. Around me the high, unearthly notes pealed out from the collection of boy sopranos, and across from me I became aware of the many deep, masculine voices joining in. I quickly glanced over and saw Anselm among the assembled monks and also another man, staring intently at me. I looked down at my folded hands and felt my stomach do flip-flops as he watched me, his eyes half-closed and a sneer on his face. I looked back at him and engaged his eyes. *Just you try something*, I thought, slitting my eyes to give him an equally cold, hard, challenging stare, until he looked away.

As I sang, I looked around at the chapel to see the frescoes covering the walls. On the wall opposite was a larger-than-life-sized fresco of Christ sitting on a throne, holding a pair of scales in His left hand. On His right, rows and rows of angels sat, their haloes gleaming gold, their faces looking quite smug, with stars and rosy clouds shining over them all. On His left, horrid, little demons were goading naked crowds of emaciated, dejected people into the open mouth of a monster. The colors were vivid, the gold leaf had been liberally used. I again had, as in the Chapel of Bones, a strong feeling of familiarity. There was some way in which I belonged here. I had been here before. I shivered and swallowed hard between singing out the notes.

The rose window caught the rays of the setting sun and gleamed like precious stones high above the west door. The vaulted ceiling was painted with gold stars on a dark blue ground. Having seen the interiors of places like this only in the bare austerity of their twentieth century remains, I was enchanted with the color and exuberance of the decoration.

I gawked at the artwork until suddenly I realized that I was the only person still standing. The boy nearest to my right side reached up and yanked on my tunic. I sank to my knees with the rest of the congregation as the priest began to intone the Latin prayer.

Afterwards I walked with the other novices around and around the cloister. The covered path ran around the four sides of an interior garden, punctuated with the doors and steps leading to the rest of the monastery. The wall was mossy where water had seeped through broken tiles in the roof. It was very quiet here, though birds were murmuring from hidden nests in the huge Yew tree in the center of the garden. Each footstep could be heard as we walked slowly around, fingering the beads of the rosary hanging from the rope around my waist, murmuring words that I hoped sounded somewhat like the paternoster I heard the boys reciting. Could I say them with enough authenticity to make the others think I know them, I wondered? I walked in a measured pattern, right foot forward, pause and touch a bead, feel its cool roundness, then left foot, pause and repeat.

As I passed the slightly open door that lead to the kitchens, I smelled the yeast of the fresh-baked bread and swallowed the saliva pouring into my mouth. I moved on slowly and breathed the smell of the wet earth. Even the smells seemed different from what I was used to, richer, darker, more intense. I tried not to inhale too deeply as we passed steps leading down to the latrines with their fetid, sulfurous scent.

Other than this file of boys saying their rosaries, there was no one to be seen in this protected place, but near the door to the chapel, a continuous chanting was dimly heard.

The rhythmic walk was soothing, calming, and my heart was slowing down from the pounding I had felt a short while before, when I first appeared in the nave of the chapel, no longer in the body of a woman, but a boy standing among the singing novices. Incredible! I was here.

Afterwards I sat crowded on a bench in the refectory with boys close on each side. The smell of unwashed bodies, unwashed wool, combined with the smell of food: turnips, some sort of coarse, cooked grain, fresh bread, was quite overpowering. I couldn't believe I was hungry. A wooden tray of bread, hacked into hunks rather than slices, was passed to me from my right. I took a piece and, as I passed it to my left, I caught out of the corner of my eye, the small, dirty hand of the boy on my right side sneaking toward my wooden bowl. "Oh, no you don't," I said, and dug my long fingernails into the thief's palm. "Ow!" he shrieked and was instantly banged on the head by the old monk, who seemed to be our keeper.

Where was Anselm? I hadn't bargained for the dirt, the smells, the little sub-plots, when I agreed to help Anselm.

I shuffled out of the refectory to the dormitory in a file of boys. Apparently the novices' bedtime was right after suppertime. We'd probably have to get up during the night for some sort of prayers. The old monk, Brother Simon, shepherded us from the rear. He pointed to the last bed in the row. "You will sleep here, Martin," he said, and watched me until I sat down on it. The bed which was mine was straw piled on a wooden plank, with a rough blanket of wool covering it. The thought of fleas made me squirm, but there was no help for it now. I lay down on the straw and pulled the blanket over me. It was the first chance I had to assess my body, to feel the changes that had come upon me. It was real. I had become a boy. I moved my hands down over my chest and hips. My chest was flat, my stomach hard, my hips narrower even than my usual slim shape. I ran my hand down between my legs and sucked in my breath. I could feel the prime emblem of my new sexual guise as though it was some external thing I was wearing. It was not that the penis lacked sensation. I could feel my fingers on it. I tried pinching it and almost cried out. I stroked it gently. Just how much of a boy was I really? Not that much, I decided. Touching it did not arouse me any more than touching my thumb would have done. I felt as though it had nothing to do with me. This was weirder than anything I could have imagined. I was still a woman, with a woman's sensibilities and a woman's consciousness. This body was a costume, and under it, or inside it, I was still Martha.

Suddenly two of the boys were standing over me as I lay curled on the bed. One, a pimply-faced boy whom I had heard called Robert, pushed me roughly on the shoulder, in the universal, time-honored gesture of picking a fight. "Stand up, you," he ordered. I looked him in the eye and very slowly swung my legs over the side of the bed and stood up. I couldn't help grinning at these kids. The other boy, named Hugh, smaller but trying to be the spokesman, said in an angry tone, "What's so funny, Martin? Don't think because your father is so rich you can get away with anything here."

"Right!" Robert joined in. "Everyone knows he sent you here to get rid of you. And if you don't want us to push your face in, you'd better give me two farthings." He reached out and grabbed my chin and shoved his own close to mine.

"Pay you? Oh it's extortion, is it?" I grabbed Robert's hand with both of mine and pushed him hard. I was was the same height as Robert. In my old body I was used to being so much smaller than almost everyone I knew, but now I still had my old strength. I shoved Robert back, throwing him off balance and into Hugh, so that the two of them lost their footing and fell onto the floor. I was immediately jumped on by four more of the boys and pinned down on my bed.

I wriggled and tried to dislodge them as I heard one of my assailants say, "We've got him, Robert. What do you want us to do with him?"

Before Robert could answer I spoke as clearly as I could. "Listen, you simpletons, I'm the best friend you ever had. You'd better not make me angry, or I won't save you from the dangers that await you." I tried to make my voice have a ring of authority, though I spoke in a low intense tone, not wanting to rouse old Brother Simon, who slept in a cell adjoining the larger dormitory room. Even to me that assertion sounded silly. It was the first thing that had come into my mind to say, but I didn't really think it was likely to impress these kids. I was surprised as the two holding my shoulders down let go and I sat up and kicked my feet free.

"What dangers? What are you speaking of?"

Now the other boys in the room entered in.

Looking over his shoulder, one boy said in a hushed tone, "He means that boy, that Roderic?"

Another, in a quavering whisper said, "They said he ran away, but I think someone took him."

Not all the boys seemed to comprehend the danger. "Don't be daft! What would anyone want with that snotty-nosed little baby?"

"All he ever did was cry."

"Especially after he came out of Brother Benedict's cell!"

"What did Brother Benedict do to make him cry?"

"Well you said, yourself, that he looked like a girl."

I interrupted. "Was Roderic the only one that went to Brother Benedict?"

Several of the boys glanced at one another, but before they could respond, we heard Brother Simon shuffling out of his cell. "Will you devil's offspring go to sleep? There will be no tart on Sunday if you keep up this noise!" He swished his stick around in the air, looking for a culprit to hit, but we had all jumped into our beds, our blankets pulled up above our faces.

That ended the confrontation, and I lay very still as I listened to the boys fall asleep. Several kept scratching themselves, but whether it was fleas or some sort of skin condition caused by their terrible diet and infrequent baths, I didn't know. My own body began to itch. I clenched my fists to keep from scratching. I was surrounded by sniffles and snores, the loudest being that of Brother Simon from his cell.

A flare thrust into an iron holder at the head of the stairs threw shadows into the dormitory and made the beams in the ceiling seem larger and further away. I heard a scuffling of tiny movements in the rushes on the floor and up over a wooden chest in the corner. Was it mice or possibly... rats! My detachment evaporated. I had no idea what year it was. Was this when the worst bubonic plague in history was about to begin? Oh God! The fear I had come here to address, that of being abducted and raped, paled at the prospect of having a rat run over me or bite me. I tried to breathe, but felt as though my lungs had shut down. It was the fleas carried by the rats that spread the disease, I now remembered. "Anselm," I wanted to scream out loud, to bring him here from wherever he was. He'd promised but he wasn't anywhere near me. I was alone.

I was going to go back to my own century, to my own woman's body, right now. What in the world was someone who didn't even like gas fires, and thought six-penny baths barely adequate, doing here?

A black shape skittered across my blanket. I jumped up. "Anselm!" I shrieked, but no sound actually emerged from my mouth.

Another shape followed it. I shrieked again. I remembered the conversation Anselm and I had in the youth hostel, totally in our minds.

"Anselm, why don't you come to me? No one else would see or hear you." My mind shaped the words clearly, but I made no sound.

I sat very still. Were the rats gone?

"Martha. I hear you, but you know I can only speak to you in your mind. We can speak silently to each other, and if you call me in your mind, I will hear it and answer you."

"Anselm, I can't stand it. There are rats! Two just ran across my bed. I want to go back this moment!"

"Of course there are rats everywhere. Now go to sleep. Tomorrow I will take you with me to the manor court. It is part of a novice's training to serve the monks in their duties."

The manor court! I fell back into the straw, rats momentarily forgotten. Oh my God! Wouldn't Will love that! Perhaps I could find out some tidbit that would revolutionize his research. But would I ever be able to get out of here and would I ever get him to believe me?

16
The Road 1348

AS THE SUN rose, Anselm and I walked along the road out of Canterbury, sometimes in mud so deep that I almost lost my shoes in trying to pull my feet free. I had hardly slept at all between the fleas and the constant expectation of more rats. Now I jumped at every shadow, felt my flesh crawl when I imagined what might suddenly dart out at me. Yet despite the condition of the road and my nervous state, I was grateful to be up and moving. The shoes I was wearing were slightly more than ankle-high and tied around the calf and again around my knees. This managed to keep most of the mud on the outside of the shoes, but they were coated beyond recognition. Anselm, wearing only sandals, soon had boots made of drying, peeling mud.

My apprehension began to fade as I immersed myself in the scene around me. The road was fairly busy with walkers and riders, most of them with large bundles on their backs or heads. Some were riding on or leading animals on halters: donkeys, cows, goats, an unwilling, bellowing ox being goaded mercilessly, while other travelers laughed and called suggestions. The smell of cut hay battled with the animal odors all about. A cow relieved herself explosively, causing pushing and shoving and much laughter as the travelers darted out of the way. One man was harnessed between the shafts of a two-wheeled cart. As he pulled it by, I could see that it was piled high with wicker coops filled with pigeons. Almost all of the people were passing in the opposite direction, toward the town. Their clothes were much like mine, woolen tunics or robes, hose, leather shoes or sandals. The women wore ankle-length skirts with shorter tunics on top and head coverings that looked like nuns' wimples. I kept turning around to stare at each passerby until one woman, without dislodging the bundle on her head, stuck out her tongue at me, waggled her fingers in her ears and crossed her eyes. I grinned, turning to walk backwards so that I could watch her walk on. I relaxed. This adventure was going to be fun.

We had arranged that I would carry Anselm's leather bag with his parchments, quills and ink and walk a few steps behind him. My job, I had been told, was to keep Anselm supplied with sharpened quills and parchment, and to mix ink as needed. As a novice, I needed to show a proper degree of subservience, but it made conversation hard, and I had so many questions. The houses in the villages we passed looked terribly flimsy, and in several instances had been burned to the ground. Most of them were little, round structures woven of thin branches, willow wands perhaps, and sealed with dried mud. Wattle and daub it was called. I had written a paper on building techniques in agricultural societies for my course on architectural history. In some houses, smoke poured from a hole in the thatched roofs; in a few it poured from any opening, even places in the walls. I had noticed red eyes on a number of passers-by, the result, probably, of living in such smoky dwellings. The general effect reminded me of pictures of dwellings in some African savannah community. Some men were daubing mud over a structure of woven twigs that was the framework of a wall. "Are they building that house or repairing it?" I called to Anselm.

Anselm looked where I pointed and smiled back at me. "Do you know of the crime of breaking and entering?" "Sure." I nodded. "Well, with houses like these, breaking in means literally that, breaking through the wall and taking what you want. That house was broken by a thief and the cottager is repairing it." I tried to imagine sleeping in a house and expecting someone to break through the wall at any moment. I shuddered. It competed with rats for creepiness.

"What keeps everyone from just breaking into everyone else's house?"

Anselm looked back at me as though he couldn't believe such a dumb question. "It is against the law! It is against God's law as well as the King's and the Bishop's and the Lord of the Manor's. And each of them will exact punishment if the law-breaker is found out."

There seemed to be no order to the villages. They had no proper streets and their houses were placed any-old-where, some with hardly a body's width between them, and others set neatly in fenced gardens. Some were of stone, but most were thatch and twig and daubed mud. Dung heaps and piles of straw, twigs and rotting vegetables, were helter-skelter all around the dwellings. It all reminded me of illustrations in my childhood book of nursery tales. I was looking at the houses of the three little pigs. Many of them certainly did look as though one could huff and puff and blow them down. Some of the villages had larger stone and timbered houses with many out-buildings, and fenced fields surrounding them. These were the manor houses, I supposed.

Before I knew what had happened I heard the pounding of hoofbeats and cries of the passersby. Then Anselm was turning and falling on me, pushing me out of the road and into a ditch. A man in armor on a horse, also in armor, came pounding by, scattering the wayfarers on all sides. Then several more. I imagined them coming towards me with lances pointed. I curled up more tightly and buried my face in the weeds lining the ditch. I felt weak.

A few people raised their heads from the ditches into which they tumbled. One man stood up and shook his fist after the disappearing riders.

I stood up. I was just brushing myself off and about to climb back out of the ditch when another armored knight thundered up and pulled on the reins so that his horse, whinnying loudly, rose up on his hind legs, his front hooves flailing at the air before he landed back on all four legs and stood quivering in front of me. The man stared at me, and then turned to Anselm who had stood beside me, his hand on my shoulder.

"Is this boy one of your novices?" the man demanded of Anselm.

"He is, sir." Anselm put his both hands on my shoulders and drew me against him.

"A fine looking lad. My lord would pay a goodly sum to take him as a page. What say you? Your abbot will be pleased with some gold." He jingled a small leather purse tied to his wrist.

Anselm, good God, you must not! I thought the words as hard as I could. But I bowed my head and looked down at my feet.

"Sir knight," Anselm spoke quietly and I could feel him swallow hard. "All such transactions must take place with the abbot. The boy's father has influence and has given the abbey a great fortune. I am only a keeper of books."

Two more knights rode up, and one shouted, "Let's go Preston, the Duke is waiting." Our questioner laughed and spurred his horse into motion and rode off.

Anselm pulled me into a tight hug. "You wouldn't have sold me to him, would you?" I was shaking. "Sell you? No. That is not what will happen." He knelt down and put his ear to the road bed and then rose. "It is safe for now," he said.

We walked on.

"Isn't it against the law to run people down in a public road?"

"Those are the knights who were with the Black Prince at Crecy. They are a law unto themselves. In France they took plunder, killed everyone, burned the crops, did as they pleased. They cannot do quite the same here, but they are often beyond the law. They are the henchmen of powerful lords hired to do their dirty work." *Like kidnap little boys?* I wondered to myself.

Anselm's voice was hoarse with anger. "We must keep our novices away from them, whatever they offer."

"Would they have really run us down if we didn't get out of the road?"

"Oh, yes. And no one would have dared to do anything. Unless we were villeins of their liege lords, and considered valuable property for some reason. Then they might have had to pay a fine. But not a big one, you can be sure."

Now was the time to ask. "Anselm, what happened to Roderic?"

Anselm did not answer. I repeated the question.

"What have you heard about Roderic?" Anselm tossed the words back over his shoulder.

"The boys were saying that something happened to him. That he disappeared after he had been in Brother Benedict's cell."

Anselm walked on, increasing his stride so that I had to run a bit to keep close behind him. Again he spoke without turning to me.

"We were told that he had run away." We walked on for a while, Anselm walking faster and faster. *What's going on here?* I thought. An image appeared for an instant of Will trying to speak to me about the rape. I couldn't speak about it to him. *That's it. It's because of his having been raped.* I felt queasy, wondering whether to continue questioning Anselm, but then thought, *If I don't pursue these things, there is no reason for me to be here.*

"Anselm, tell me about Brother Benedict."

"Brother Benedict? What do you want to know about him?"

I felt my fury burning up inside me. I reached forward and grabbed the rope fastened around Anselm's waist so that he was forced to halt.

"Damn it, Anselm!" I shouted, "Do you want my help or not?"

Before he could answer, out of the corner of my eye I was became aware that an old man in a broad-brimmed straw hat was coming along, riding astride a donkey. The beast was so small that the man's knees were up higher than the saddle. Still holding Anselm's rope belt, I turned to look at him and grinned. He looked so silly. But before I could move out of the way, he raised the stick with which he was goading the donkey and brought it down sharply on my hand. "Ow," I shouted and dropped the rope and grabbed my smarting hand.

"Brother, shall I beat that disrespectful boy for you?" The old man raised his stick again, climbing off his donkey and walking threateningly toward me.

Anselm grabbed my shoulder and pulled me out of the way. He held up his hand. "Thank you, old man. Bless you. You are kind to offer, but I will discipline the boy myself."

Reluctantly the man lowered the stick, "Mind that you do. There is nothing worse than a disrespectful boy." The old man rode off muttering to himself. "If he was my boy, I'd have the hide off him. Those monks are too soft with them."

I sucked on the welt raising up on my wrist and wiped away the sudden tears that had come with the blow. Anselm shook his head ruefully and let go of me.

"Anselm, you've got to tell me everything you know, or suspect, or I am going back to my own life." To myself I thought, *please let me be able to.*

He nodded. "Very well. Let us sit here." Once again he pulled me off the road and onto an embankment surrounding a field of some kind of grain, barley, perhaps. Sitting down, and gesturing for me to sit too, he pulled a piece of dried meat and a small loaf of bread out of his bag. He divided these equally between us and took a bite of the meat before speaking.

"You are quite right, of course, but it pains me terribly to speak of these things. Please be patient with me and I will try to tell you what I know." He looked down at the food in his hand, then out at the passers-by, anywhere it seemed than at me. He spoke in a strained voice.

"You know that we take a vow of chastity. That means trying to not have any carnal desires, much less giving into them and performing carnal acts. But the devil tempts us sorely. As he does every human being. Some of us beat ourselves. Some wear shirts made of stiff horse's hair or straw to be reminded of the danger. Some of us pray unceasingly or jump into cold water or starve ourselves, all to vanquish the devil and destroy such lusts.

"But there are those who make unholy compromises. They have convinced themselves that carnality only means lusting after women. Boys and men are not within the meaning of the stricture. In a community of men, such intercourse between men would require mutual consent, and if it did not exist, the one desiring it would be exposed in his sinful desires." He started to shake and could not go on speaking for a moment. He swallowed a sob. He spat out, "But boys can be used with impunity." Then he said very softly, "Particularly if the man hurts the boy or frightens him sufficiently that he will be afraid to reveal anything for fear of worse pains."

"So Benedict used Roderic like that and threatened him against revealing what had been done to him."

Anselm turned away from me, but I could see his shoulders heaving. All these years that I had hidden my own terrible experience, sure that I was unique. I wondered how many people I had known had been violated in the same way. This dirty secret - why didn't people stop these monsters who did this?

I spoke to Anselm's back. "And that is what happened to you? Was it one of the monks who is still here?"

He wiped his eyes with his sleeve. "No, with me it was Godwin, the man who was Abbot at that time, and he died for his sins. At least I think so. He disappeared and was never seen again."

"So maybe having all that happen to him would be a good reason for Roderic to run away."

"He-did-not-run-away." Anselm spoke slowly and firmly, his jaw held stiffly so that he spoke from between clenched teeth.

"How do you know that?"

"He had left behind his cloak, his shoes, and his tunic. Apparently he had gone to the garderobe and was never seen again. The doors are all locked and only some of the monks have keys. And it was a bitterly cold snowy night.

"There had been a fresh snow fall, and a horse's hoof-prints could be seen at the kitchen door the next morning."

I didn't want to hear what he was saying. A vision of those knights in their fearsome armor filled my mind. "But does that necessarily mean..."

"Yes, Martha, it does necessarily mean that someone took Roderic and someone in the Abbey conspired in the taking."

"But Anselm, surely others suspected this also. Didn't anyone say anything?

"After my experience with Abbot Godwin I have no trust of Abbots, but I know better than to challenge authority. This Abbot said he had run away." Anselm held his hands palm up before him and shrugged his shoulders, looking sheepish.

"How spineless of you! No wonder you were punished!"

Anselm closed his eyes and sighed. He nodded, "Yes, you speak the truth of it."

17
The Village Court 1348

THE VILLAGE OF Ramsgate Overbrook was certainly over a brook. During the long walk, my hose and shoes had mostly dried out and the mud flaked off. I couldn't decide whether to let my shoes and stockings get soaked while wading across, or remove them and walk barefoot on the half-submerged, manure-covered stepping stones. I saw Anselm remove his sandals, so I did also, as we crossed over to reach the churchyard, where the court was to be held. *Yuck!* I thought. *I wonder how many people are infected with hookworm from walking around barefoot in all this dung and mud?* I couldn't wait to put my shoes back on, sitting on a stone mounting block to do so.

"Come along, Martin. It will not do to be so fastidious, we have work to do."

At a long trestle table under a chestnut tree, the Lord of the Manor's reeve, John Fletcher, sat with several clerks. Behind them stood a bailiff with an upright staff, its top surmounted by a wooden knob. Sitting on benches, overturned buckets, and even on the ground, were twelve men of the village. They were the jury, whose job, Anselm told me as we approached the churchyard, was to give the assent of the community to the judgments handed down by the reeve.

"They really don't have to decide anything. They merely have to approve whatever the court decides."

"Can they refuse to approve?"

"It would never occur to any of them to do so. Being a juror is an honor." Anselm drew himself up and became very solemn as he said the word "honor."

"What benefit does the juror get from this honor?"

"Well, they are given respect. Even when the court is not being held, jurors hold themselves to a higher standard of behavior and morals than others in the village. The reeve himself was one of the most prosperous of the freemen of the village, and he was chosen by the villagers."

"Really!" I had never dreamed that the Middle Ages had that degree of democracy, until Anselm spoke again.

"Of course they were not offered any other candidate."

Anselm sat down at the end of the long table and I sat on the ground just beside him. "Anselm," I asked, "I know that I am to sit here on the ground near your feet so as to give you the writing tools when you ask for them, but what is it that you will be doing?" He leaned over to me and whispered "Martin, keep your voice down. My job is to record all payments of rents, fines and fees to be sure that the Lord of the Manor gives the Abbot his share of the takings." I pondered that for a moment, wondering why the Abbot got a share. I pulled again on Anselm's garment, but before I could ask him, he quickly whispered, "Ramsgate Overbrook is a part of this manor, and the Lord is a vassal of the Abbot of St. Martin's."

Standing in murmuring bunches all around the perimeter of the court were the other residents of the village. A voice shouting unrecognizable words from beyond the crowd drew my attention, but the press of bodies was too dense for me to see. The reeve beckoned to the bailiff and he strode toward the noise, his staff over his shoulder. The crowd parted to allow him to pass. I could see a man in stocks, his face contorted by the angry words he was shouting. The bailiff hit him on the head with the staff and then on his knees, so that the man cried out and then subsided. I pulled on Anselm's robe. What had the man's crime been, I wanted to ask him. But Anselm shook his head and held his pointing finger to his lips.

The reeve nodded at Anselm. "Welcome, brother. Now that the Abbot is represented, we may begin." He struck a mallet on a small piece of wood and called out in a loud voice, "May the Lord God bless us and help us to do Justice in His name. The court of the manor of Lord Michael of Oglesby, held this twelfth day of April, in the year of our Lord 1348, in the village of Ramsgate Overbrook is now in session."

I was interested to see that Anselm took from his own bag a small abacus, which he placed before him on the table. As each villager brought his rents, payments, fines, and heriots up to the table, the reeve would proclaim the value, and the clerks and Anselm recorded the name of the villager and the amount paid. The complicated economics of the transactions were astonishing. I couldn't, at first, tell whether the amounts were arbitrary or required extensive knowledge of the value of goods and properties and the circumstances of the various individuals. Fletcher was illiterate, I realized, but he held volumes of facts in his head. "John, son of Alain, owes rent of one sheep, value of half a shilling, for two virgates of brookside lower plowland." Anselm, deftly flicking the abacus, announced, "The Abbot's share is tuppence, to be paid as one measure of barley or two of rye." The reeve then intoned, "What says the jury?" And the jury would rise, remove their caps and say, "Aye." If there were no dissent by the parties to the cases, Anselm and the other clerks would repeat aloud in unison what had been done and record it on their parchments. At one point Anselm held out his hand toward me and I handed up a freshly sharpened quill to him. He took it without saying anything. "Oh, you're welcome," I whispered. Anselm looked down at me and raised one eyebrow in an otherwise expressionless face.

Occasionally a villager would contest the assessment, saying that his harvest was too poor to support such an amount. Sometimes the reeve would challenge this, reminding the man that he had reaped enough to buy his wife a feather bed. Other times he would reduce the amount requested.

One woman, fined for brewing ale illegally, wept that she did not have the four pence and did not see such an amount from one harvest to another. The reeve looked her up and down and said, "We'll take your cloak." And the woman sniffed, nodded tearfully, and removed a rather substantial-looking black woolen cape from her shoulders. She did not seem upset to surrender this garment, and I wondered if, on such a warm spring day, the woman had worn the cloak for that purpose. Sometimes the reeve would argue the relative values of the goods claimed on behalf of the Abbot. Then he and Anselm would debate examples of what similar items had brought this past six-months at the market fair at Canterbury, or whether, indeed, the items were similar.

"That bull was old and past his prime, it cannot be compared to a fine young beast like this one."

"True he was old, but he has sired scores of fine offspring and farmers still come from far and wide to pay for his services."

The day grew warmer and the watching crowd more restless. Now the rents had been paid, the fines for transgressions levied, and it was time for the criminal proceedings. The man in the stocks, Alfrey, was brought before the reeve, his hands tied before him and his feet dragging chains attached to two large and heavy stones. The bailiff stood just behind him, the knob on his staff held a few inches above the prisoner's head. One of the reeve's clerks rose up and surrendered his seat to the village priest.

"Call the accuser," the reeve said in a clear voice.

A woman came forward, knelt before the reeve and swore to the priest that she would be truthful, then stood before them, her head bowed.

"Tell us what you saw, Bertha, Robert's daughter." The reeve spoke in a flat, almost uninterested, voice, but the villagers moved closer, not wanting to miss a word.

"I heard a funny noise coming from the byre, your honor, when I was bringing some straw in for the milk-cow's breakfast." Bertha spoke slightly above a whisper, and kept her head bowed.

"Tell us what sort of noise. And lift your head, that all may hear you."

"It was a laugh, like. A woman's voice, I thought. Like someone was doing something that was sneaking fun, but with something over her mouth, so she would be kept quiet."

"And then what did you see?"

"Oh, your honor, then I saw my Maudie," here the woman's voice shook, "her what was promised to the miller's son, with this great brute of a man on top of her, and both of them with their bottoms bare."

My eyes grew wide and I looked up at Anselm with the beginning of a grin, but he was staring down at his parchment, his face totally without expression.

"Did you know the man?"

"His face was covered with his hood, so I couldn't see his face, but he was a great brute, with his great privates sticking out." The villagers whispered and tittered, and the bailiff waved his staff around shouting, "Be silent!"

"Then what?"

"I shouted, 'Get away from her, you great fornicator!' and he grabbed up his stockings and ran from the byre, and I called down the lane, 'Oh stop him, stop him. He's stealing her virtue and I've already paid the Lord her marriage fees.' Then began the hue and cry, and all the folk on the lane ran out of their houses and began to chase the great brute. And I want that man to pay me back those fees. Thinking he could get it for free, the whoreson!"

"Step aside, Bertha. I will call the leader of the hue and cry."

"Call Fergus."

One of the jurors stood up and said, "Here I am, your honor."

Fergus was duly sworn as well. "Tell us what happened, Fergus."

"I was just finishing eating my morning bread, your honor, when I heard Bertha, here, shouting 'Stop him' so I ran out and all the other good folk came out and we grabbed up our rakes and hoes and sticks and started running and shouting through the village, looking in barns, and sheds, and byres, and raising a goodly noise."

"Did you know where to look? Did you see a man running away?"

"No, your honor. We just went in the direction that Bertha pointed but we didn't see anyone, until we came to the miller's grain shed, and then behind some sacks of barley, we found this one (pointing to the prisoner) skulking."

"The girl bewitched me. I'm a god-fearing married man," Alfrey shouted and was bopped on the head by the bailiff. He subsided into snuffling and murmuring, "I never would do such a thing, else. My wife won't let me have my rights. The girl wanted it. And it wasn't for free!"

"Cut off his privates!" shouted a drunken voice from the crowd. A loud buzz of assents and arguments began in the crowd, with several of opposing points of view beginning to pummel one another. "To suggest such a thing! Cut off your tongue, you anti-Christ," shouted someone in answer to the first shout. "We're a Christian folk, we don't do such things!" And another villager called out, "Look who's suggesting such a thing. Davy Thatcher! It's a wonder that your privates haven't worn off from humping maids." That brought the crowd to a roar of laughter.

"I will have order," shouted John Fletcher, jumping to his feet to see who the people were, saying such unseemly things, "or we will adjourn to the hall, and none of you will be allowed in. For shame, would you give Ramsgate Overbrook the reputation of Vikings and barbarians?" The crowd quieted down, and Alfrey's continuing whimpers about his innocence because of being tricked could be heard.

"What is the usual penalty," I whispered to Anselm. He shrugged. "He will certainly have to pay the girl's marriage fees and will doubtless be whipped soundly into the bargain."

"What are marriage fees and why is it such a big thing?"

Anselm leaned back and smiled down at me. "The liege Lords make their money from fees paid them. A couple wishing to marry must pay the fee. For a man and woman to couple without paying for the privilege is a form of stealing from their liege."

"And the woman? Is she also penalized?"

"If it is established that she did, indeed, bewitch him, she could be burned for consorting with the devil. But that is not likely. Instead, she will be considered a less worthy marriage prospect. Therefore she will command a smaller marriage portion and a smaller fee. For that reason, her mother wants part of the money she paid returned and the Lord wants redress for the loss of his money. In any case, the girl will be put in the stocks as a warning to other women to shun harlotry."

I returned my attention to the proceedings, fascinated to see how it would be sorted out.

Now the reeve addressed the prisoner. "What is your name?" The man told him. "You are not from this village. Where do you come from?"

"Farthingdale, your honor. But I am innocent." The crowd laughed.

The reeve looked Alfrey up and down. Far from being a "great brute" he was a small, undernourished man, his legs bowed with the rickets, hardly coming to the bailiff's shoulder.

"Are you a villein? Who is your lord?"

"Sir Michael Ramsey, your honor. I am one of his cottagers. I do whatever I am told. I labor by the day whenever I can get the work."

"Does your work include being in a village not your own, and skulking in a miller's storehouse?"

Alfrey hung his head.

"Why did you come here, Alfrey?"

Alfrey mumbled something, but the only word that I could discern was "barley."

"Speak up!" demanded the reeve.

"I was sent to buy a sack of barley," Alfrey said more clearly, though his head hung even further down on his chest. "And that girl, Maudie, said they had one in the byre."

"How did she happen to tell you that?"

"Why, I said how blue her eyes were, and would she give me a sip of water. And as I drunk the water that she bewitched, she asked me what I was doing in a village not my own, same as you just did, your honor. And then the spell was on me and I said I had money to buy some barley but I would give her the money if she would let me see her..., you know. And she said they had barley in the byre and I could come in and get it from her."

"We'll have to question the girl as well. Bring her forth."

At this Bertha began to blubber and shout and it took some minutes to discover that Maudie was gone. No one knew where. I could tell from the knowing looks that passed among the villagers, that no one was surprised by this, not even the reeve. Turning to Alfrey, the reeve asked, "Will Sir Michael go bail for you?"

"I don't think..., I don't know, your honor."

"Lock him in the cellar of the Hall until we can speak with Sir Michael."

Just then the hammering sound of a horse's hooves could be heard on the road and visored knight splashed across the brook and drew up before the reeve's table. Reeve Fletcher pushed back from the table and stood very straight. "I have a message from the Duke for Lord Michael," said a somewhat muffled voice from inside the helmet.

"Lord Michael is away for this day, Sir Knight. But I am his man. May I take the message?"

The knight pushed off his gauntlets and extracted a rolled parchment from within one of them. He pushed the visor off his face as he leaned over and handed the parchment to the reeve. I saw that it was the knight who had tried to buy me on the road. Anselm drew in his breath sharply. He put his hand on my head. The motion attracted the knight's attention. He looked over at me, sitting on the ground and smiled, or rather grimaced, with his clenched teeth bared. He pointed his index finger at me and then rubbed his fingers together as though caressing coins. He turned his horse's head toward the road and rode off without saying anything more, while all the crowd looked hard at Anselm and me.

"John Fletcher, we must finish these proceedings," Anselm said firmly, "else the gates of the city will close before we can get back."

I was really frustrated as we walked back to Canterbury that neither Anselm nor I would ever discover what became of Alfrey, or, for that matter, Maudie. There was no plan for Anselm to go to Ramsgate Overbrook until the following year, and it would have caused talk if he started asking people about the matter.

"Martha, there is no one I COULD ask!" It amazed Anselm that I kept at him about it. For me it brought home more forcibly than anything else how isolated and insulated village life was in these times. Perhaps Will could find some reference in the records of the manor court, assuming he could ever find those particular records, assuming that I could ever get back to him.

18
Monastery Life 1348

I WAS BECOMING used to life as a teen-aged boy in a monastery. I was so fascinated by everything around me, the speech, the clothing, the work, the agriculture, the rituals of the canonical day, that I was, for the most part, able to forget the lack of sanitation, the smells, the vermin. This was amazing, as I had always been squeamish about cleanliness. My college friends teased me about having been toilet-trained too early. I was usually too tired to even worry about fleas and rats when I got into bed.

The one thing I could not become accustomed to was the sparse and tasteless food. I was naturally thin, but I had always enjoyed food, seeking out exotic tastes as different as I could find from the genteel Southern cuisine of my childhood, where Sunday dinner was inevitably roast chicken and peas. My classmates and I in New York would try out a different ethnic restaurant each weekend. Once we had gone to a fair at the Cloisters, a museum of medieval art in northern Manhattan, and had sampled the foods purporting to be from the period: meats roasted on spits, pieces of sausage called salmis, pasties, tarts, plum puddings, sweet meats. There had been jugglers and Punch and Judy booths. The whole thing was delightful and delicious. It was nothing whatever like my present surroundings and the stuff I was consuming now. Words like pap, gruel, mush, mess (as of pottage), glop, gunk crossed my mind as hunger forced me to refuel with what was offered, mostly boiled unsalted grains cooked to a paste and occasionally seasoned with onions, or some root vegetables with a few slices of hard-boiled egg or some scraps of stringy boiled meat. The bread was coarse and gritty. I suspected that if I were to continue to eat it for very long, my teeth would be ground down by the dust of the millstones in the flour. I often had to swallow several times as the awful food resisted going down my gullet. I found myself dreaming of tossed green salads with watercress and sliced navel oranges, of crispy fried chicken with biscuits, of glazed Chinese spareribs, of hot fudge sundaes drowning in whipped cream - almost anything with fat and protein and fresh fruits and vegetables.

It was curious that, though I had changed so that I possessed the physical parts of a teen-aged boy, I had maintained my modern woman's health and body awareness. I was becoming even thinner, though the constant walking, gardening, running errands, even kneeling and rising in the parade of religious rituals throughout the day kept me strong. I had been athletic all my life: a tennis player, a swimmer, a canoer, and had even taken a wonderful course in jui-jitsu in college, which had done much to relieve my constant fear of being physically abused. That sports training and being relatively healthier and more fit than they were, allowed me to best the boys in most of their rough-housing and games.

Now I was using different muscles, and after the first day's aches, not really suffering physically, though hunger pangs accompanied much of each day.

The boys with whom I spent my time had accepted me, though they were made uncomfortable by my unwillingness to participate in the pranks that seemed to be their chief entertainment. "Come on, Martin, if you don't help us get this bucket of slops hung up over the door, we'll know that you mean to tell Brother Simon." Feeling as I so often did that I was playing a part for which I was writing my own script, I had gotten up and placed my hand on the crucifix hanging on the wall over the storage chest. "I swear by my Patron, the holy and blessed Martin, and by my Lord Jesus that I will never tell anyone what you are doing," I intoned in a solemn, even sepulchral voice. "But you're going to clean it up when it falls," I shook a finger at them. They had been duly impressed by my performance.

"You know you'll rot in hell for all eternity if you don't keep your word," Robert told me, his voice shaking a bit. He was so pale with concern that his pimples stood out red and angry. I had merely stared at him impassively, my eyes narrowing, until he looked down. The boys had given up playing tricks on me. That they were impressed by my mysterious allusions to the dangers that they faced and my ability to save them from what lay ahead of them, never ceased to surprise me.

I concluded that they were more frightened by the disappearance of Roderic than they had seemed at first. I was just strange enough for them to believe I had the powers I suggested I had. I was one of them, yet somehow apart. To the boys I seemed to be a sort of camp counselor, and some of them had begun to bring me their problems.

"Martin, I have been given the choice of working with Brother Stephan in the infirmary or with Brother Hart in the kitchen, and I don't know which to choose."

"Do you like them both the same? "

"I suppose so. But once I choose, that will be my work for all time, and what if I find later on that I don't like what I chose?"

I put my finger to my lips and my chin in my hand and pondered. What did I know about such things, anyway? The boy was looking at me so hopefully.

"Well, let's think about it in another way. What is it you like about each job?"

After comparing the relative pleasures of feeding the brothers on the one hand and of curing their ills on the other, and the relative distresses of butchering chickens and seeing people bleed and die, without a clear direction becoming apparent, in desperation I sent the boy to pray for a sign. "Just keep praying until you have a vision of one or the other, then you will know that is the one to choose." If you prayed long enough would anyone get a vision? I had no idea, but it seemed more appropriate advice than tossing a coin.

I was pretty sure that several of the smaller boys had been the recipients of Brother Benedict's attentions. He turned out to be the man with whom I had had a staring contest at that first choir practice. And I thought he was the man who had accosted me in the privy on my first visit to the fourteenth century. On two separate occasions I had been walking with one of the boys when we had encountered Benedict. Both times my companion had stiffened and remembering something he needed to do, had dashed off in the opposite direction. I had stood at my full height, looked the monk directly and challengingly in the eye, and said loudly, "Good day to you, Brother Benedict." The monk was the first to look away each time, smirking to himself and mumbling his reply. In keeping with the role I was playing, I forced myself to engage in these little tests with Benedict, but each time we stared at each other I felt hairs rise on my neck. I was fully expecting he would try to do something to me as well.

19
Will's Worry 1952

"I MIGHT NOT come back," she had said. And he, like an idiot, had said "I might not be here." What a dumb thing to say! He punched a pillow. He wanted to punch a wall, or bang his head on it. What an idiot! He should have grabbed her and held her here. How could he have let her walk out that way? But even as he thought that, he knew that wouldn't have worked. He'd just be another guy who abused her, treated her like dirt.

He hopped up and walked back and forth across the room, straightening the posters on the wall. Maybe she'd come back any minute. Maybe she just needed to make a gesture and then would think better of it. He stared at the Arc de Triomphe. They were going to go to Paris for the Christmas break. Would they get to see it now? He stooped to smooth the bed-cover, dried the few dishes and put them away. He ran a finger over the inside of a cupboard and noticed black grit - soot from the "killer" fogs that had been bedeviling London.

Will indulged in several hours of self-justification: she was nuts, she didn't know when she was well off, there weren't many men who would put up with her craziness. He had been patient, hadn't he? He did his share of the housework, maybe more than his share. He respected her as a colleague. What was so terrible about his wanting her to enjoy sex as much as he did? Nothing! Normal people had sex because they enjoyed it. People who loved each other had sex because they loved each other. And he did love her. It wasn't just sex. She was funny. She was smart. They were interested in the same things. They were best friends. But without her fully participating in sex, it was like a big chunk had been taken out of the marriage. She just was not normal, that's all there was to it.

He threw himself down on the bed and punched the pillow again. He rehearsed every scene he could remember ever since their wedding and their sailing for England, trying to find the thing that had tipped their relationship from fun to a great big blank wall. But he kept coming back to her saying that she had been raped and the terrible sobbing and the shutting down after that revelation. Had she thought he would reject her if he knew? That he would think she was damaged goods? He had heard of men having that reaction, but how could she think he was like that? He had been having waking nightmares in which he saw some guy on top of her without his being able to help her. The visions reduced him to a shaking, sweating state.

The agonized fury and tortured thinking had eventually turned to worry. She hadn't taken very much money with her. And hardly any clothes. Where was she going to stay? Was she going to meet some other man? Once, weeks before, when he was pondering what to do about their sexual problems, it had occurred to him that with someone as uninterested in sex as Martha was, he didn't need to worry about her leaving him for someone else. But maybe she was just not interested in HIM.

Then he worried about her being warm enough, being sick, losing her mind and not knowing who she was. That seemed a real danger when he discovered that she had not taken her passport with her.

He tried to force himself to study, but the words swam away from the page. He decided to clean the flat and pulled everything out of cupboards, washed everything, put everything back. He laughed at himself, wondering why he did this. Martha would be surprised when she came back... if she came back. *Please, please let her come back.* He went outdoors and walked for hours until he was thoroughly lost and had to hail a cab to get home.

Finally he fell into bed in complete exhaustion and found he could not sleep without Martha in the bed with him.

He spent several days like this, days in which he listened for every noise in the street, every footfall in the hall, hoping every moment that it was Martha coming back. For five days he lived on coffee and chocolate bars and almost no sleep, not seeing anyone, speaking only to himself. When he started to have the shakes and be unable to pick things up without dropping them, he realized that he would have to do something or he would become seriously ill.

He forced himself to eat two of their rationed eggs, two slices of toast, a banana, and a pint of milk. He still felt ill and he looked horrible. He took a quick bath and shaved five days growth of beard. Then he threw his things into their other knapsack and took the next train to Canterbury.

Hopping off the train, he stood outside the platform gate as the other passengers rushed past him. He had no idea where to look, what to do. Maybe he should retrace their steps, revisit the places they had gone to together. So once again he found himself walking down St. Martin's Lane, this time on a cold rainy day, with a biting wind in his face. Coming upon Mr. Cooper's house, he stopped and tried to decide whether to knock on the door. What would he say? He tried out, "Mr. Cooper, have you seen my wife?" "Mr. Cooper, my wife has left me and she said there was someone in Canterbury who could help her. Was it you?"

He was standing there shivering with the wind and wet, when the door opened and Cooper came out, with a small yapping dog on a leash. The dog strained to reach Will, barking furiously, and at the same time, practically turning itself into a knot wagging its tail. "Hello, there, young man. Are you lost? Can I be of assistance? Chaucer, behave!" Mr. Cooper yanked on the leash and the dog sat down, shivering and whining softly.

"Mr. Cooper," Will now felt very stupid. "Um, do you remember me, sir? Will Morton. I was here in the autumn with my wife, and you showed us the Chapel of Bones."

Mr. Cooper, wrapped in a trench coat, peered at Will from beneath an Irish tweed slouch hat. He shook his head frowning with concern. "Sorry, old chap, you must have me mixed up with someone else."

"No sir, it was you. You were mowing your grass, and you stopped and walked us down there," Will pointed to the end of the lane, "and you said you thought there might be a way for Martha, that's my wife, to get inside the Chapel of Bones."

"This is most peculiar, young man. I would never take anyone to see the old chapel. I don't even like to walk Chaucer in those woods. And I certainly don't encourage strangers going down there. Just what are you up to, anyhow?"

Will turned and put his hands over his eyes, feeling an alarming dizziness. He tried to take deep breaths. He pulled out a large handkerchief and blew his nose, wiped his eyes and the rest of his face. He didn't know why Cooper was denying all this, but it was evident that he wouldn't get anywhere arguing with him. "Sorry I bothered you, sir," he mumbled as he turned to walk back down the lane.

"Just a minute, Mr. ah, Morton was it? You don't look well. Let me take Chaucer over to the road for a minute and then come inside and I'll get you a cup of tea."

Will stood there defeated and miserable. "Thank you, sir." If Cooper had told him to stand on his head, he would probably have complied.

A few minutes later, seated on an overstuffed, plush armchair in front of a very hot coal fire, Will felt a bit better. Mrs. Cooper, a stout woman in a brown tweed skirt and mustard-colored twin sweater set, came in carrying a tray with two cups and saucers, a small brown teapot, hot water, and milk and sugar. Mr. Cooper followed with sliced fruitcake, two cake plates and two paper napkins.

"Thank you Mrs. Cooper, Mr. Cooper, you are both very kind. You shouldn't have troubled." But he was very glad they had. Will helped himself to the cake and accepted a cup of tea after saying, "Yes, please," to the various choices: sugar, one spoon? milk? Do you prefer it strong? As he bit into the cake, he realized that he was famished again. He reached over and took another piece. Mrs. Cooper left them, trilling in a high voice, "Woman's work is never done."

"Now, what is all this about?"

"Well sir, my wife and I came here looking for the Chapel of Bones and we met someone who looked and sounded just like you, who was mowing the grass, and who offered to show us the Chapel. And..." Will stopped.

"And what?"

"And my wife left home about a week ago and said that she needed to go to Canterbury, because there was someone here who could help her, and I haven't heard from her, and I thought she might have come to you, ...or whoever it was we spoke to, because you, I mean this man, said he could get her into the Chapel."

"Does your wife often do things like this?"

"No sir. She never did it before."

"Let me tell you something, Mr. Morton. I never go to the Chapel and I certainly don't encourage anyone else to go there. People are always reporting seeing ghosts there. A lot of nonsense. That building is very old, and very fragile. I'm hoping the trees and bushes grow up and hide it so that no one goes there. It is too isolated and would be a perfect place for undesirable types to... um, do undesirable things. Probably gangs would come to divide up their spoils. People start going there and, the next thing you know, it'll be a tourist place with car-parks and tea wagons.

"I've never seen you before, and I never told your wife that I would get her into that Chapel. Now the only reason I am speaking to you, aside from the fact that I have rarely seen anyone look so miserable, is that you are not the first person in the last several months who has told me something like this. A friend from Tyler Hill, fellow I bowl with, wanted to know why I walked right by him in Woolworth's without saying hello. I thought he was stark raving. I never go into Woolworth's. I'd rather die than go into Woolworth's! Even my wife wanted to know why she had seen me sitting on the grass when there were so many weeds in the dahlia beds. I said, 'Are you mad? You know I never sit on the grass.' And she said, 'But Algie, I saw you.'

"So there is some chap going around impersonating me, and I want to know who he is, and why he is doing it." He leaned forward and stared intently at Will. "If this is some sort of scheme, you'd better come straight out with it, or you're going to be in a lot of trouble."

Will stared back at Cooper, his mouth falling open. This was really too much. "If you don't think having my wife disappear isn't trouble enough...," he began angrily. "Look, I don't know who we spoke to. If there is a 'scheme' as you call it, I'm as much a victim of it as you are."

Cooper sat quietly looking at Will for a long minute. Then he slapped his thighs with his outstretched fingers and said, "I don't know why, but I believe you. So now what are we going to do?"

"I guess I'd better go to the police and file a missing persons report. Then I'm going to go to all the places we went to together and see if anyone saw Marti in the last week. And, um, maybe I'll get up some posters to put around with her picture on it. I don't have much money, but maybe I'll offer a reward or something."

"Where do you live? I mean when you are not searching for your wife?"

"I'm doing postgraduate study at the University of London. We have a bed-sitter in Clapham South."

"And where will you live while you are going around with your posters and inquiries?"

"I don't know." Will had not given it a thought. "Maybe the youth hostel. Perhaps I could find a room somewhere. Is there a YMCA?"

"We have a guest room. You shall stay here. That way you can tell me what you've been doing and if you've seen my doppleganger again. And I will keep an eye on the chapel, in case Mrs. Morton or anyone else appears there. Do you have a photo of her? I know a great many people in this area and perhaps I can help with the search."

Will looked around the warm, homey room and suddenly felt his despair ebbing.

"Mr. Cooper, I don't know why you are being so kind to me, but my mother always said, 'Never discourage a generous impulse.' So you've got yourself a guest."

He reached out and shook Mr. Cooper's hand.

In the morning, as Will ate a huge breakfast, Cooper phoned a number of people in the area to ask if they had seen Martha. None had. Mrs. Willingham remembered both Martha and Will perfectly, but had not seen them since last October. "But now that I recall, they were asking about you, Algie."

"Now what about this photo of your wife, Morton?" Will handed over the one he carried in his wallet. "We'll get this blown up. I'll take down the particulars and take it around to the printers. I think 50 copies should do it, don't you?"

20
Set Up 1348

ON THE LONG and tiring walk back into Canterbury after the Manor Court, I asked Anselm what to do about it if anyone tried to molest me. But all he would say was, "You will know what to do."

I tried to ask how I would know, running to catch up to his long stride and grabbing at his robes. But he shook his head and I realized that the passing peasants, coming back from market in Canterbury were looking at me disapprovingly. As we passed through the gates of St. Martin's, he said again, "You will know when the time comes," and he turned toward his own quarters, leaving me to find the file of novices being shepherded into vespers.

"Martin," the quavery voice of Brother Simon pulled me from the line, "Tomorrow you will help in the kitchen garden. The Lord has blessed us with an abundance of beets, and we need extra hands to harvest them. You will report to Brother Seraphim right after Lauds, and you will work all day without interruption until the sun sets. Your food will be brought as you work." I bowed my head and merely said, "Yes, brother," but I could feel the hair on the back of my head tingling. For some reason I was being singled out. Without the other boys or Anselm, I was being set to work alone.

As I moved toward the table, Robert crowded in close to my back and whispered, "They've got me too. Do you know why just the two of us were chosen for this?"

We sat together at the end of the bench, so tightly together that our shoulders touched. I glanced sideways at him and saw a line of sweat slowly proceed down his cheek.

"Don't you know who Brother Seraphim's superior is?" he whispered. I thought that Robert must really be concerned to risk violating the silence of the meal. I looked at him sideways and shook my head ever so briefly.

As Robert bent his head to repeat the blessing over the food, he uttered, "Benedict," from the corner of his mouth and almost closed lips.

"Amen. You may eat," the Abbot intoned. I took up my bone spoon, but struggled to get the porridge to stay swallowed.

By sun-up the next morning Robert and I were on our knees in the sandy kitchen-garden pulling up what seemed like endless rows of beets. The work went slowly as each beet needed first to be loosened with a small trowel, care being taken not to bruise the fat root, nor could we pull them out by the tops since these also had to be kept intact. Then the beet was to be brushed off with a feather so that the soil would be preserved in the garden, and each vegetable placed in its basket according to size. Brother Seraphim, true to his name, was gentle and patient, but relentless, making each of us do the job over and over until it was just right. "No, no lad, like this. The dear Lord made these beets and we must care for them as the blessings that they are." The sun was high in the sky before he allowed us to work unsupervised, by which time my tunic was sodden with sweat.

I raised up on my knees to stretch and loosen the muscles in my back and neck. The small shed that held the garden tools caught my eye as, for an instant, I thought that I had seen something move across it's unglazed window.

"Robert," I said softly, "Do you feel like we are being watched?"

"Of course, dunce," he was not enjoying this work, "Brother Seraphim hasn't taken his eyes off us for a moment."

"No, someone else. Someone over in the garden shed."

We both sat back on our haunches and looked at the shed. Just before Brother Seraphim came running back toward us with a gentle admonition to keep at the work, "Not time to rest yet, dear lads," I was sure I saw the door of the shed move slightly.

I bent back to the work and then moved to where I could speak softly to Robert. "I think it would be a good idea if neither of us were ever alone."

He looked hard at me and bit his lips. He replied, "A very good idea."

As the sun descended, we were released from our labor and went to wash our soil-covered hands at the lavabo on the cloister wall outside the refectory. Most of the community had already attended vespers and had filed into the dining area. Anselm stepped out from between two pillars and said, "Martin, I wish to speak with you. Robert, go to your supper."

"I, I, cannot, brother. Martin and I have taken a vow to do everything together."

Anselm raised his brows and looked questioningly at me.

"Brother Anselm, would it serve if Robert stood over there near the door to the refectory so that he cannot hear your words but can still see me?"

Anselm gave a mirthless chuckle and shook his head. "It will serve." He positioned himself so that Robert could see me but the monk's back was to the boy.

"Is this arrangement to protect you or Robert?"

I was surprised by the question. "Oh, I wasn't thinking of myself. I thought my task was to find out who is abusing and stealing boys and stop them. I've felt so much that I was play-acting that I stopped thinking about being in danger myself."

Anselm's answering smile was rather grim. "You are very bold for someone who has always lived in fear."

"Yes it's not like me at all, is it? But since I am playing, being someone other than myself, I can do things I would never do in reality."

"You must not be too bold, and above all, don't be foolish. You are the bait. It is up to me to stop all of this, with your help, of course. But do not make it more difficult by making yourself unassailable. Tonight you are to sleep in the Westgate. I have something I must do at St. Peter's church. I will be away most of the night, so be very careful. It is possible someone will make an attempt to get you. I think it will not happen until I come back just before the cocks crow."

For the first time since assuming this persona, I felt not disgust, nor squeamishness, nor annoyance, but the steel band of fear constricting my chest. I had been trying to figure out, since I came into this time and place, exactly what Anselm wanted me to do and when I would have to do it. Anselm's response to my questions had only been to continue to say, "You will know when the time comes." Rats were horrifying, of course, but they were a threat one could see. Suddenly I realized, with mounting panic, that although I could speak to Anselm in my mind, ever since I had been here I had not experienced my real gift. I did not know what would happen in advance, I could not see what had happened in the past. Of course I had never been able to do it on command, but now I just seemed not to be able to do it at all. That was even more frightening. "Anselm, what has happened to my ability to know things? I haven't had it since I have been at St. Martin's."

Now Anselm looked alarmed. "You must try. Think hard about what is to happen."

I shook my head. "That never works."

Anselm looked down at me, his eyes filled with concern. "Think hard, think about tonight, about being in the Westgate Tower. What do you see?"

I did what I was told, shutting my eyes and trying to evoke an image. I thought of the Westgate as Mr. Cooper had described it, with candle flames going down the outside of the tower. Instead, I saw a monk spread-eagled out on a stone slab in St. Peter's church.

"Why are you going to St. Peter's and why are you lying there on the floor?" I asked.

"There, you see! You can see things that will happen. This is the night I go to give thanks to St. Augustine for the manuscripts. Martha, if this is to work, if I am to right my wrong, we must do everything as it was done before."

"Wait a minute." I grabbed his arm. "I was just remembering the image that I saw when Will and I were in St. Peter's that time. I still think I have lost my gift. And I have questions. What do you mean bait? What am I supposed to do? And why the Westgate? How could I keep 'it' from happening? I don't even know what 'it' is. Anselm, you are not making any sense. I don't like this. I'm going with you to St. Peter's."

Anselm detached my hand from his arm. "No, Martha, it is something I must do alone. And you will have to do this next part without me. You have come so far. You have done so well. Please help me now, or I cannot go on. This is the time for you to do something very courageous that will heal you as nothing else can. Please. Go now and eat your supper."

I turned, my shoulders hunched forward, a terrible sense of foreboding making me feel weak, and walked slowly to where Robert was waiting for me.

"What were you and Brother Anselm speaking of?"

"Could you not understand any of what we were saying?"

"No, but I could tell that you were not speaking to that brother as a novice should speak to his elder. And I heard him say your name strangely, as though he had a lisp, 'Marthin'. But I have never known

Brother Anselm to lisp. In fact, I have never heard him say much of anything to anyone. You must know him well."

I thought *I don't know him well at all, so why do I keep trusting him as I do?* I shook my head. "Let us go in or we shall have no supper."

21
The Westgate 1348

AT SUPPER THAT evening after the beet harvest, Brother Ranulph the Abbot's secretary, came to the novices' table just as we were finishing our meal. We all jumped to our feet, pushing back the rough-hewn benches on which we had been sitting. The movement caused the candles in the middle of the trestle table to flicker. "Good evening, Brother," we intoned in unison.

"Lads, Brother Simon has taken ill. His head is very hot, and he coughs painfully. He has gone to Brother Caritas for treatment." We all bowed our heads, put our hands in a prayerful position, and said, "Jesus bless him and keep him." As surreptitiously as I could, I reached back to grab the crust still on my plate. Several other boys did the same and Ranulph frowned at us, but let it go unremarked.

"It is, therefore, necessary," continued Ranulph, "for you to be sent in groups of two or three to new temporary sleeping places, so that you may be supervised by various brothers. He pulled a scrap of parchment from his sleeve and began to read names from a list in his hand. "Stephen, Edgar, and Wilfrid, you are to go with Brother Thomas. Gilles and Coram, you are with Brother Alfred." He continued down the list, coming finally to, "And Martin and Robert, you will go with Brother Benedict to the tower of the Westgate." *This was it,* I thought. And while my mouth went dry, I was excited at the prospect of seeing inside the Westgate when it was relatively new.

"Oh sweet Jesus, what can we do?" Robert's fear was murmured in my ear. I smiled slightly and shook my head.

"Pray for strength," was all I could think to say.

Benedict appeared and said, "Which are the lads who are to go with me?"

The refectory began to darken as the lay brother who tended the tables blew out the candles. I watched as he came closer to ours.

I had a sudden urge to hide under the table, but I stood up, forced myself to look him in the eye again, and said, "I am one, Brother, and Robert is the other." Benedict raised his eyebrows as though this was news to him, nodded and said, "Well, wait for me outside in the cloister. I shall be along in a while."

• • •

When Will and I had first done the sightseeing rounds of Canterbury, I had been particularly taken with what was left of the city wall. The Westgate was still used as the main entrance to the city, though the portcullis, the huge iron gate that hung over the road, was never lowered any more. We learned that there had been six gates in the city wall for as long as there had been a city wall, since late in the third century AD, when Saxon raiders had threatened Canterbury. The thought of a structure, so marvelously old, still being in use gave me shivers. The Westgate was the largest and most important of the gates, since it connected to the main road to London. I bought every pamphlet that the gift shop had for sale. So I learned that by the 14th century the gate, and the chapel that had sat on top of it for hundreds of years, had become so dilapidated that a new gate was constructed in the place of the old one. But instead of a chapel on top, the new building had a circular defensive tower on either side of the roadway, its gun ports facing outward from the city toward any potential attackers.

On the ground level of each tower was a circular room with a fireplace. Above the gateway itself was a large hall, reached from the roadway level by a winding stair in the north tower, and above that, two more rooms leading out onto battlements.

I made Will listen as I read all this information and pointed out the fascinating facts. "You see these recesses on the top of the wall? They are called machicolations and they are made specifically for dropping boiling oil and boulders on invaders."

"Yech," Will said.

The portcullis gate could be raised into the main room above the roadway (where it lodged still,) and lowered at sunset to protect the town. Travelers striving to reach the city before sunset had to spur their horses to a "Canterbury pace" from which the word canter derived. Oh, how I did savor all these bits of information!

St. Martin's Abbey nearby was reached from the tower by an external door in the second-story room, a sturdy flight of stone steps leading to the wall and then another narrower set of steps to the Abbey grounds. These last were barred with a stout locked iron gate on the city wall. Nothing of this remained in the 20th century, but it was certainly the place where I had seen the monks with candles when I fainted outside the Chapel of Bones.

What our guidebooks had not told us, however, was that some of the monks had been quartered in the gatehouse, while new dormitories were constructed on the Abbey grounds to accommodate the growing community of St. Martin's. The novices usually slept in the main building of the Abbey, in a large room above the library.

• • •

As Benedict walked away, I said to Robert, "We are going to have to help and protect each other." The boy bit his lip and nodded, forcing back tears. Robert and I sat on the low wall separating the cloister walk from the garden at its center and watched our fellows being led to other parts of the Abbey by various monks. I looked up and saw Robert, his blemished face more serious than was his wont, staring at me. "Martin, I can't believe that Ranulph didn't scold us over the bread. Is it true that your father is the richest man in the kingdom? That must be why you are favored. You don't act haughty and proud as I would expect of a rich man's son."

I didn't know what I could say without revealing more than was safe. I shrugged. "Perhaps your expectations are at fault. I am a person like any other."

"No, you are different from any boy I've ever known. I know you are brave and strong, Martin. You were not afraid of any of us, even when we all jumped on you. You seemed to think it funny. Sometimes I think you are more like a parent than one of us. I was the leader of the boys before you came. I was prepared to fight anyone who would try to take my place. But somehow the boys look more to you than to me. I look to you as well. And even if you were not so strong, I have no desire to fight you."

I smiled, "Oh what a relief!"

Robert bristled and looked as though he did have a desire to fight. "Now I think you mock me."

"Never! I meant only that you would be a strong adversary. I would prefer to have you on my side. Robert, you obviously suspect Brother Benedict of evil motives, as I do. What do you think will happen tonight?"

Robert pulled me closer to him so that his mouth was almost at my ear. He lowered his voice to a whisper: "Well, you know that several of us think that when he takes boys into his cell, he does evil things to them." I nodded. "It is always the smaller boys, and they refuse to speak of it when they come out, but little Edmund wept and whimpered for nights after he had been in with Benedict. You and I are among the older boys, so I don't know what he intends to do, but if he tries to do anything that I don't like," he came even closer to me and lifted his tunic very quickly to reveal a small sheathed dagger on a narrow girdle at his waist, "I am prepared."

I drew in my breath sharply. "I wish that it may serve you well. Better still, I wish that you have no need of it."

But I thought sadly that such a tiny weapon held by a half-grown boy was unlikely to be of much use.

"And what do you think," I whispered, wondering if I should speak of this. Robert looked at me and waited for the rest of my question. "What do you think happened to Roderic?"

Robert looked away and swallowed several times. He cleared his throat and wiped his brow, though it was not particularly warm. When he finally spoke it was in such a tiny whisper that I had to lean forward to hear. "I think there is someone outside of the Abbey who likes to perform sinful acts with boys. And I think, God forgive me, that there is someone inside the Abbey who arranged to steal Roderic for that purpose."

I gave a harsh mirthless laugh. "I have the same suspicions. I think that whoever is doing this inside the Abbey is being well paid for it. No one would risk such a thing otherwise."

"And you think it is Benedict?"

I nodded, then held my finger to my lips as a door in the cloister wall creaked open and Brother Benedict appeared, carrying a large roll of heavy cloth and a pitcher. He smiled at us. "So we are ready now. If one of you could... Here, you are very strong, I know." He shoved the cloth at me. "Carry this for me. And you, " he held the pitcher out to Robert, "carry this, but don't spill it. It is some fresh warm milk from the evening's milking to help you sleep in these new surroundings. This way I can have my hands free to unlock the gate."

We walked up the steps to the wall and then up the tower steps, where Benedict inserted another large, iron key from a ring hanging on his belt and allowed us to enter. I nodded to myself as I realized that this was the door through which the apparitions I had seen, when fainting, had come. Inside we were in a small circular room into which the interior steps from the ground floor rose. On a shelf near the door stood ten candleholders with fresh tapers.

Seeing me staring at them, Brother Benedict said, "Those are the candles we use when we go to Matins. I will prepare two more for you lads to carry." Another arched doorway brought us into the hall of the Westgate.

I looked around with open curiosity. This was an example of 14th century architecture, untouched by the renovations and changes of later eras. It was simple, unadorned and built for the ages. A large fireplace stood on one wall and on the opposite a window looked out over the city. The floor was covered with rushes which deadened the sound and gave off a pleasant grassy scent. On the side walls partitions had been erected to allow four monks to have tiny cells. Two of them had curtains drawn, their occupants having already retired. "Are there only four brothers sleeping here?" I asked in a soft voice, turning to Benedict.

"No, four more sleep in the rooms above. And two are in the ground floor room of the other tower. This one," he pointed to the cell closest to the door, "is mine. And you two will sleep on the rushes in front of the fire. I have brought this cloth for you to lie on."

"Who sleeps in the remaining empty cell?" I needed to know that Anselm would be close enough.

"Brother Anselm has that one. But he is away all night tonight, and he often works until late at his reading and writing." Benedict drew two sewn leather cups from under his robe, poured the milk into one, and handed it to Robert. "Now let me see you drink up, so that I know you will sleep." As he turned to fill the other cup, Robert held up his cup and sniffed at it. He caught my eye and shook his head very slightly. I nodded once, just as slightly. As Benedict handed me the second cup, Robert cleared his throat and moved toward me, his hand pointing beyond me, saying, "Um, Martin, do you see..." Before he could finish his sentence, he had tripped over his own feet, spilling his milk, and falling into me causing me to spill mine as well.

Benedict, his face a spasm of fury, hissed, "You stupid clumsy ox!" and began to beat Robert about the head with his fists. Robert raised his arms to ward off the blows and took them instead on his hands and on his chest. I was afraid that if he got his hands free, Robert would reach for his dagger. I pushed my way in between them, receiving some of Benedict's furious punches on my own body as well. "Brother, Brother, please, we will clean up the milk. Do not disturb yourself so. We are sorely tired from tending beets all day. We will sleep without the milk. Please Brother, stop."

Finally my words got through Benedict's rage. He controlled himself with difficulty, taking a few sobbing breaths, before he subsided at last. He pointed to where the milk had soaked into the straw on the floor and said through stiff lips, "Throw the wet part into the fire and take some dry floor covering from under the window. Then go to sleep." He went into his cell and drew the curtain. We could hear his bed creak as his body was lowered onto it.

As Robert and I unrolled the cloth and spread it over the rushes, I mouthed at him, "Don't go to sleep." He nodded.

For what seemed like hours, I watched the firelight playing on the vaulted ceiling. As my eyes grew heavier and heavier, I struggled to keep awake by making shadow pictures with my hands on the ceiling. A rabbit, a wolf, a goose with an open beak, these I could remember from one unhappy summer at camp.

"I wonder what Will is doing now," I murmured to myself. I wished he were here with me, holding me, kissing my head. Protecting me? No, tonight I would have to protect myself. And now, for no particular reason that I could name, I felt certain that I would not come to harm.

I imagined Will's naked body without feeling the least embarrassment. That's one thing that living in a community of males does, I thought. There was a fair degree of modesty among the brothers, but there were many opportunities to see men unclothed, in the privies, in the baths, without it being the least bit unseemly. But then there was no sexual interest for me in seeing either the men or the boys. Will was another story. I thought about him lying on our bed preparing to give me a "sex lesson" and I smiled. In my mind's eye I traveled down his long torso, his muscular arms covered with golden hair, his strong chest and such narrow hips, more brown-gold at his pubis. I remembered the feel of his body beneath my lips and felt warmth in my own body and a sort of longing I had never felt before.

I had begun to doze off when one of the monks who slept in the room above appeared and called clearly, "Rise brothers, it is time for Matins." Slowly, from all the occupied cells, from the floors above and below, men appeared, yawning and stretching. Since they slept in their clothes, no time was needed for dressing. They formed a single file, herding Robert and me into line with them, and each of us took a candle, which was lit from one burning near the door. As the file of men and boys emerged from the outer door and onto the stairs, all of us began to chant softly in Latin and continued to do so all the way into the chapel, where we joined the rest of the community in this middle-of-the-night worship. The low chant grew louder and as we settled to our knees in the dimly lit chapel, we began to say the Paternoster in unison, touching our beads for each line.

Returning to the Westgate and our beds, I whispered to Robert, "If anything is going to happen, now is the time."

"Martin, why do we stay here, waiting for who knows what? Let us just go. If we go very quietly down the steps to the ground level, we can throw the bolt and open the door to the roadway."

"You go, Robert. Why should you have to be here? I am required to stay and wait. But this does not have to involve you."

"I don't understand. Who requires this of you?"

"I have made a vow if you like. I must stay here to help end this evil."

"By being stolen?"

"If that is what is required."

"Well then, I will hide below in the gateway. Then if Benedict tries to steal you, I can, I can... get help." He pulled his little dagger from around his waist and put it in my hand. I was about to refuse it, but I knew that Robert was giving me something precious to him. "Thank you, my good friend," I whispered and tucked it into my waistband.

As I looked at him, Robert seemed to grow before my eyes. There was a determination in him that had not been there before. I reached out and grabbed Robert's shoulder. "Robert," I whispered into his ear, "Tonight you will prove yourself more than a leader of boys. You will be a hero!"

He stared wide-eyed at me and then straightened up to his full height. He grasped my hand briefly and then, piled the straw to look like a body in the dying firelight, and ran noiselessly down the stairs to the circular room below.

I lay listening for the creak of Benedict's bed. I had my back to his cell so that he would not see my eyes open when he emerged. I heard nothing, then felt a horrendous blow to my head. My last conscious awareness was of a choking feeling as a cloth was placed over my face.

22
After Him 1348

IT WAS PAST Matins and all the rest had returned from the early service to their beds for a few more hours of precious sleep. Anselm used the large brass key to let himself into the northern drum tower and thence to the dormitory above the Westgate of the City wall. A distant cock crew, but none nearer by had started yet.

Everything was precisely as it had been that other time. The small round chamber was completely black, but he had seen the stair in the faint light from outdoors when the door was open. He needed only to walk straight ahead to reach the bottom step. The circular steps were completely regular. He would put his hand on the wall of the staircase and he could feel his way up them in total darkness. In any case, the topmost part would be illuminated by the single candle burning in the upper room and a lantern was on the stairwell about half-way up. As he walked forward carefully, the hairs on the back of his neck gave him an uncomfortable sense that everything here was not quite the same after all. He stood still and listened.

The barest hint of a sound, a tiny breath perhaps, or a heartbeat, suggested that someone was in the room with him. For a moment he was in confusion about what to do. Perhaps it was his own pounding heartbeat that he had heard. In any case he had waited too long for this opportunity. He had to go ahead, and he did, feeling for the first step and then the second, almost tripping from the weakness in his legs. "St. Augustine, help me," he prayed, but without audible words.

As Anselm began cautiously to climb the stair, noticing how still it was within the strong walls and how his own bare feet were almost soundless, he heard a muffled indefinable noise from above him and another below in the street, that one the creak of a horse's leather. He pulled himself into a niche cut into the wall and waited to apprehend the person coming down. "Martha, is it you?" he asked in his mind, waiting for her to tell him exactly what had happened. There was no answer. The flap of sandal on the step preceded a very large hooded figure descending slowly and carefully, one hand balancing the figure's bulk on the inner coil of the steps. Now a labored breathing as of one carrying something heavy and as the figure passed under the dim lantern, Anselm could see that whoever it was carried a large bulky roll of cloth over his shoulder and the roll gave out snuffles and muted noises, whimpers or perhaps moans. It sounded like a young boy or perhaps a woman. He could not see the monk's face, for surely the person was a monk, hidden in the deep cowl of his habit. Nor could he identify which monk it was by size or girth.

Nevertheless, he was certain it was Benedict. As the man and his burden came abreast of him he reached out his trembling hand to stop him, then put his hand down again. Perhaps it was not Martha in the roll of cloth. He held out his shaking hand again, but could not make it work. The person continued to the bottom of the step. Anselm felt the overwhelming shame of his indecision. Was this never to end?

Still hiding in the niche, Anselm heard the door at the foot of the tower open and heard a bridle's jingle. He could barely make out the bundle being handed over. A few undecipherable whispers, then the door closed and the hooded figure turned up the stairs, moving with greater ease.

Suddenly Anselm heard Martha's voice in his head, very faint and garbled, but he heard his name and the words, "Help me." He sprung up and dashed down the stairs, no longer caring if he made noise, and threw the bolt on the door. A small hand reached out and grabbed his habit as he was passing through the doorway. "Brother, please help. He took Martin." A boy's voice gave a sob and quickly inhaled. "I think, I think, he went that way." Anselm recognized Robert in the faint light. "A man in a shirt of mail. Walking, leading the horse. Martin all trussed up over the saddle. He couldn't, couldn't go very fast that way." Robert took a deep breath and spoke more calmly. "I'm sure we can overtake them."

They hurried out into the main street of the city, stopping to listen for a horse's hooves, but they heard nothing. It was so still, that they could hear the river on the other side of the city wall. A hanging sign over a nearby tavern began to creak as a slight breeze came up. Far down the street a shutter at an upper window opened and a faint voice cried out, "Gard'leau," as the contents of a chamber pot hit the street. There were many side alleys and small cobbled lanes leading off, none of them straight, and the twists and turns would muffle any sounds. "Martha, where are you?" he spoke aloud and Robert looked at him strangely. "The gate is locked, so they must still be in the city." To cover his misspeaking Anselm said, "And if they are inside the wall, we will find them."

"Brother, I think I know one place where they could get out," said Robert. "At the end of Pound Lane there is a drainage opening that goes under the wall. Perhaps they could get through that."

"How could they? That leads into the river and, in any case, one could not take a horse through such an opening." But he had no idea which way to go, and in mounting panic, began to walk down Pound Lane, Robert barely keeping up, with Anselm's long stride.

Pound Lane was called this because animals left untended in the streets of the city were impounded there until their owners reclaimed them and paid a fine. Anselm and Robert could smell the animals as they heard grunts and rustles of the horses, donkeys, pigs, and dogs curled up or standing in the roadway.

At the turning in the lane they heard the sound of running water and found a barred opening, where a small tunnel passed under the wall. The sky was becoming less dark and some poultry quite close by began to offer sleepy crows and cackles. Robert squatted, reached out to the iron bars covering the opening, and found them loose, sitting against the hole but not fixed into it. "Brother, look. This tunnel is not closed. A horse could not pass through, but a person could."

Just then they heard some muffled splashing, as though oars were being dipped into the water. Pulling the bars away, they plunged into the dank opening, immediately stepping ankle-deep in the filthy water trickling into the river. Anselm could feel the water creeping up his robe. He shuddered. A few steps in a crouched position and they were at the other side of the wall and there the surface of the river was a foot or so below the floor of the tunnel. Dimly they saw something moving on the other side of the narrow channel. A small boat was bobbing there, its occupants, if any there had been, were no longer in it. The river, crowded between walls, moved briskly along.

"They must have come out on the other side. We shall have to swim, Brother. I don't know how else to catch up to them."

"Robert, I don't know how to swim, and the current is quite swift here."

A log bobbed close to where they stood, but did not seem to be moving with the current. "I think that log is for mooring the boat on this side of the river. We can pull it free of the rope that holds it, and you can grab it and kick your feet. It will help you get across to the road on the other side. I can swim." The boy looked most solemn, but he was obviously proud that he could do something the older man could not.

Once again Anselm was doubtful. The water so deep and swift. Perhaps this was not the way the person who took Martha had gone. Could we be going in the wrong direction and risking our lives? Perhaps thief was already at the Cathedral close, or hiding in the city. "I don't know, lad. We may be in error here. We must not be too hasty."

"Brother," Robert was so agitated his words tumbled out through shuddering breaths, "if we wait, m, m, m, Martin might die!"

As he was hearing Robert's urgent, almost hysterical voice, Anselm suddenly heard another voice, this one in his head. "Anselm, Anselm." It was Martha's and it was quite clear and firm. "They are taking me to the Chapel of Bones." Anselm drew a deep breath and squared his shoulders. He placed his hands on the boy's shoulders. "You are right, you wise boy. Help me pull the log free."

A few minutes later, pulling themselves, chilled, breathless and drenched onto the opposite shore, they began to walk quickly down the London road. A horse's hooves could be dimly heard in the distance. Anselm imagined that it was plodding slowly along, as though heavy-laden.

"Come along. I think that they are going to the ossuary at the farm," he said to the boy, quickening his pace.

"Really Brother, what makes you think so?"

Anselm did not answer for a moment. He pondered what to tell the boy. "No one goes there very often unless there is a burial, so it would be a good place to hold someone prisoner, and people could go in and out without being seen. The spring planting is done, so no one is working there at the present time."

"I pray you are right."

23
Abbot Godwin 1348

CONSCIOUSNESS SLOWLY RETURNED. I was being bumped up and down. My head throbbed. With each throb tiny flashes of rainbow lights sped across the interior of my eyelids. I was not able to tell if I couldn't see because I was blinded or in a very dark place. I could blink my eyes, but everything was still completely black.

My head hung down on one side of something moving and my arms were tightly restrained against my body, crossed over my stomach, so that the weight of my body was on top of them. Something hard pressed between my stomach and my right wrist, and I remembered shoving Robert's dagger into my waistband. When I tried to speak, I could feel that something was over my mouth, but not my nose. I could breathe, after a fashion, but each inhalation caused fabric to be drawn against my face. I realized that my lack of vision was a blindfold wet with my own tears, not a loss of eyesight.

Slowly I became aware of the sound of horse's hooves moving in perfect timing with the thing underneath me. As I tried to thrust my body to one side, a hand pushed me back to my original position.

I thought of the foul cloth Benedict gave us to spread on the rushes in front of the fire in the Westgate hall. It must be wrapped around me now, with a rank smell that told me I must have retched into it.

In my mind I called out to Anselm. "Help me!" I said, but heard no answer. Where was he? Why did he not reassure me? I felt a wave of anger. "Stupid man!" I thought. Why had I trusted him? And then an even more intense wave of despair made me go completely limp.

The horse stopped and two arms lifted me down, flipping me over so that I was supported under knees and neck, though still immobilized. Most of my body was on the ground. My head and shoulders were lifted and dragged along. I felt cold wetness seeping into the lower part of the cloth around me. Before it was able to saturate the whole of my covering, I was placed on something hard that rocked and bobbed, and I heard the sound of paddles being dipped into water.

I had no idea how long I had been unconscious. I was in a boat now. That meant I was being taken out of the city while it was still night and the gates still closed. The river, if that was indeed where I was, flowed by the wall in the north and west of the city near to the Westgate. If I had not been taken far, then I was unconscious just long enough to get me from the Westgate hall to the riverside.

While the boat was still rocking I was lifted again, and for a moment of heart-stopping terror was sure that I was to be tossed into the water to drown. "Martha, where are you?" I heard Anselm asking, and sighed with relief, about to tell him "at the river," when I felt myself lifted onto what could only be another horse. The air was fresher here. Beyond the horrid cloth I could smell growing things.

I heard a man's voice. "There will be no one on the London road yet this early so you should be able to get there without being seen."

Then another. "Were you followed to the drain?"

The voice closest to me replied. "No, I don't think so, and Benedict went back up into the tower, so even he doesn't know which way I went."

"What did you do with the horse that brought this one to the riverside?"

"I just turned it loose. In Pound Lane there are so many beasts that one more won't be noticed for some time."

The horse started to move. "We're safe. No one will look for him among the bones." Three different laughs could be heard, two of them farther away now.

The horse began to plod along, stopping every few steps to shake its body as though trying to dislodge its burden. "No, you don't, old fellow," said the voice. "You've got a job to do and so have I." The next time the horse gave a violent shake and a whinny and twisted its rump from side to side, I could hear a swish in the air and a smack on the horse's flank. "You walk nicely, or you'll get more like that," the voice said.

I marshaled my thoughts so that I could communicate clearly. "Anselm, Anselm," I called inwardly. "They are taking me… to the, to the Chapel, Chapel of Bones."

My head continued to throb and all of my limbs were numb. Continuing waves of nausea contributed to the prolonged misery. I was going to die. First they would use me sexually, then I would be murdered. Was that what happened to poor Roderic? And what could I do about it? I didn't have much faith in Anselm arriving like Sir Galahad to say, "Unhand that maiden, or lad!" or... whatever!

I wriggled my fingers to combat the numbness. As the blood began to return to my hands, I began to concentrate on reaching the small dagger at my waist. It was too small to be of much use, and I had never used a weapon, but perhaps I could surprise my captors with it.

• • •

By the time the horse stopped and hands reached to take me from its back, I had worked my right hand to my waist. I could even feel the dagger through the cloth of my tunic. I could not, however, get my tunic raised high enough to actually grasp the weapon. But quickly I was carried from the horse and placed on my back on a flat hard surface.

"Is he awake?" an older harsh voice asked.

The voice of the man who brought me answered, "We shall soon see." He fumbled with the cloth around my head. A strip of cloth was removed from my eyes and I could see a candle flame and a strange face looking at me.

"Stand back my lord, he's puked on the cloth around his mouth."

The harsh voice spoke again. "Keep the rest of him tied up for the moment. I want to speak to him before we take all of his bonds away."

The man washed my face with a wet cloth, raised my head up and held a cup of water to my lips. "Listen, boy, and do what you are told." He turned my head. I saw a tall, gaunt, white-bearded man staring at me. He leaned over and gazed into my face.

"What is your name?" he said hoarsely.

I couldn't speak. His eyes were black and lifeless as stones. He held my gaze as though he would see into my head. I swallowed several times and finally whispered, "Martin."

"You have a pretty face, Martin. Benedict chooses well. He and I have similar tastes." He chuckled and was overtaken by a rheumy cough. When it subsided he continued in an even more choked voice. "Now if you do exactly what I say, you will not come to harm. In fact, you will have a better life than you could ever do in a monastery. But if you oppose me, you will die. Do you understand me?"

I tried to slide my tunic up under the cloth that still imprisoned me from the neck down. My right hand kept firm hold on the dagger as my left slowly inched the fabric upwards. After a long time I nodded my head.

"You will be unwrapped and untied. You must lie completely still and not move, except as we tell you to. Do you understand?"

Again I nodded.

The younger man began to untie the ropes which allowed the cloth to loosen somewhat. As he worked on the ropes around my ankles I finally got my tunic up to where I could grasp the hilt of the dagger in my right hand. As I was rolled onto my stomach I was able to ease it into my hand, and slip it up into my sleeve before a pull on the cloth turned me back again, face upward.

Freed at last from the horrible cloth, I remained flat on the floor, waiting to see what would happen next. The little structure which I had known as the Chapel of Bones was larger inside than I had remembered, with shelves built on the walls. There was a not-unpleasant earthy smell. Focusing on one shelf near me, I was not surprised to see a skull and a pile of bones. Then as I turned my eyes I could see more parts of skeletons.

The man who had been untying me turned to look directly at me. I drew in my breath sharply. He was the knight I had seen during my walk into the countryside with Anselm. Over the chain mail shirt he wore a tabard with an insignia of a noble house. Three gold castles with three gold keys on a ground of scarlet.

He smiled at me as he registered my shocked recognition. "Well, well, my lad. You've come to us after all."

The older man spoke. "Preston, go and get some food from the saddle bags for the lad. I will examine him before our long journey." He leaned toward me.

"Stand up, Martin. I would look you over. You are what, twelve years old?"

I nodded.

He smacked my face in momentary fury. "When I speak to you, boy, you must answer 'yes, my lord.'" He growled. "Surely you know that."

"Yes, my lord." I stood up very shakily, falling back on my knees several times as the circulation returned to my legs. I held my right arm close to my body so that the dagger would stay in my sleeve. Where must I stab to do the most damage? The blade was only about six inches long. Could such a blade penetrate a man's heart, even if I knew exactly where to strike?

"Come here, boy." The man sat down on a carved wooden chair with arms. I walked slowly over, willing my feet to move. He grabbed my shoulders, and pulled me against him, enclosing my thighs with his own. I could feel his hot breath on my cheek. Smell the stale perspiration of his clothes. He began to stroke my flanks, then reached under my waistband and grabbed my boy's penis.

I could stab him now, I thought. As I started to pull the blade down my sleeve, I heard Anselm's voice in my head.

"Martha, I am nearing the ossuary. Are you in there?"

"Yes," I thought to him, leaving the dagger for the moment where it was.

The old man closed his eyes to slits and smiled slightly as he rubbed and pulled on my alien sex organ. "You do not respond. A pity. Ah well, I am too old to do anything more than feel. I will leave it to your new master to teach you what you need to do." He released me and grabbed my chin. Turning my face, he said, "Ah, little Martin, shall I tell you what will happen to you?"

I am not really here, I thought. *This is not happening. I am a twenty-five-year-old woman. My name is Martha Davis Morton. I live in the middle of the twentieth century. My husband's name is Will Morton. I am a architectural historian. My name is Martha…*

The old man smacked my face. Harder this time. "I asked you if you wanted to know what will happen to you?"

I bit my lip. "Yes, my lord." The candle flame surged and flickered then burned steady again.

He ran his finger around my eyes. "Your eyes will be painted." He stroked my cheek. "Lovely, not even the hint of a beard yet. Your cheeks will be rouged. You will be dressed in wonderful clothes." He stroked my buttocks. "Clothes that reveal your delicious young hams. Oh, you will be very beautiful. You will wear furs and jewels and live in great luxury. And do you want to know why?"

I don't think I can stand any more of this, I thought. *I am going to vomit again. I must do something to make him stop.* But I answered, "Yes, my lord."

"There is a very great man. A fighting man. His troops besieged Paris. He captured the Dauphin and brought him back to England for ransom. He owns castles in France, in Burgundy, and many lands in

England. He is immensely rich and powerful and..." he leaned forward and rubbed his lips on my cheek, turning his head from side to side as he did so, "he likes boys. Not men. Not women. Just boys. And when they are no longer boys, if they have served him well, he gives them a fortune and makes them his vassals. You will like him and he will like you."

"Is that what happened to Roderic?" I heard myself ask, unable to keep the anger from my voice.

"No, Roderic was fool-hardy. He refused to do what he was told. He was punished for it. Learn from his example, Martin."

My eye was caught by a spot of bright light that suddenly shone through a hole in the parchment over the window. The sun was coming up. It formed a bright circle on the wall next to the old man. For an instant it was black again and then shone once more, as though someone had passed by on the outside. I felt a gleam of hope. Anselm!

As my captor kept up his stream of obscene descriptions, I answered, "Yes, my lord," at appropriate intervals and thought to Anselm, "Are you right outside the chapel?"

"I am here." Anselm answered me. "Robert has gone around the wall to see if he can see in from another window." With the full rays of the sun on the parchment, I saw the dark outline of a man as though in a shadow-puppet show. "Ah, I hear him coming now." Then another shadow appeared to one side, moved toward the first and seemed to blend with it.

"Oh Jesu, it is one of the knights," Anselm cried out, "he has a sword pointed at me!"

Very faintly, as though I was only imagining it, I heard a man's low voice say, "Don't move, monk, or I will run you through." I forgot to say, "Yes. my lord," when I realized that I not only could apprehend Anselm's thoughts, but even the things people said to him. A smack across my face reminded me, and I quickly said it.

I heard the other voice say, "Who are you and what do you want here?"

Then Anselm's stuttering, "I'm a member of the order that owns this farm. I have a right to be here. Why do you threaten me?"

"I have no need to threaten you, monk. I shall simply kill you."

My hand felt the point of the little dagger. "Don't let him, Anselm," my mind shouted. "Get away from him. Kick him. Put your finger in his eye. Be brave. Don't let them take another boy!" I began to jerk and twist my body as I tried to rally Anselm, causing my captor to hold me even more firmly.

"What are you doing, boy?" he shouted in my ear. "Are you having a fit?"

"He's thrown me to the the earth." Anselm was giving me a second by second narration of what was happening to him. "He has raised his sword over my chest! Oh my God, help me. Oh St. Augustine, I have dedicated myself to you. Help me. Oh dear Jesus..."

"Roll out of his way, Anselm," I urged, rolling my own body as the old man kept smacking me, as though by my own motion I could inspire Anselm.

"Please God. I want to rest,"Anselm whispered, "I don't want to wander the earth any longer. I shall be brave in Heaven."

"No Anselm, you promised to save me! " I shouted these words aloud. "Remember your promise!"

"Who are you speaking to, Martin?" The old man smacked me hard, causing my head to snap back. "What is wrong with you?

Anselm's words thundered in my head. "I have kicked him down. Now I am stomping on his sword hand. God has indeed made me stronger than this knight."

I heard a grunt and then a thud outside. Then silence.

My body sank against the old man's chest in despair. It was all over now.

The old man could not see who entered, only hear the door creak as it opened slowly.

"Ah, you have come back, Preston. Help me tie up this mad lad again. He is throwing himself around in a very strange manner. And get ready for our journey." Not hearing an answer, he turned, still holding me tightly and we both beheld Anselm standing in the doorway, his face and clothes covered with soil and bits of grass, holding a sword in front of himself with his two hands. "Abbot Godwin!" gasped Anselm, staring open-mouthed at the old man. "I thought you were dead these many years."

Godwin jumped to his feet and pulled a gold-hilted dagger from his belt. Before I could get my own dagger into position, he grabbed me and pulled my arms behind me so that I was facing Anselm. He held both my wrists in one hand, his blade against my throat.

"Do not move!" he growled into my ear.

Anselm held out his sword, moving into a crouch.

"Who are you, Brother?" said Godwin. "And why do you threaten me with a sword?" I held my breath as I could feel the knife begin to press into my throat.

"I am the chronicler of the Abbey of St. Martin's." Anselm spoke in a low firm voice. "I am called to end the depravity that you began."

Godwin's grasp tightened around me and the blade, pushed a little harder into my neck, began to burn.

"Well, the first result of your calling will be seeing me slit this boy's throat. So stand back and put up your sword." He held me even more tightly. "And I think that is not your sword. It is Preston's. What have you done with him?"

"He cannot help you. A brave lad who was with me, a friend of Roderic's, dropped a heavy stone on his head. Now unhand that lad."

24
Daggers Drawn 1348

"YOU CANNOT HURT me, Brother Chronicler. I will kill this boy, but his body will be my shield." Perspiration dripped onto me from the old man's face. As his fierce embrace of me tightened, the pungent smell of his body became stronger.

"You may indeed kill him, but I am in front of the only door. And I have the sword."

"Which I doubt you know how to use. If memory serves me, swordsplay was not part of the training of novices."

"Keep him speaking, Anselm." I thought the words as clearly as I could. My head was forced downward so that I looked directly at the soft leather of the Abbot's boots.

"Nor of abbots, Godwin. I suspect we are fairly evenly matched. I have sent for help. You will not escape."

The image of the wiry Nisei instructor at Columbia came to me. "Now this is something you would never do in a fair match," he said, standing behind me, his arms holding mine tight against my sides, "but if one of you small women ever needed to get out of the grasp of a rapist or a mugger..." I stared at Godwin's feet, one on either side of mine. Keeping my upper body as still as I could, I lifted my right foot and smashed it down with all my strength on the instep of his right foot, and instantly kicked back up again with my right heel into his groin. He yelped and then coughed and I could feel his grasp of my hands loosening. Pulling them free I shoved my back against him with sudden hard force, and as I did so, turned my whole torso. Godwin's dagger slashed first across the skin of my neck and then sank into my shoulder. Despite the pumping gush of blood seeping warm into my tunic, despite the burning pain, I pulled the dagger from my sleeve and pushed it into Godwin's chest as far as I could make it go. He screamed something unintelligible and grabbed at the blade with both hands. As he stood there swaying, Anselm came quickly forward and held the point of the sword against Godwin's adam's apple. I felt my vision fading and the floor coming up very slowly to meet me.

• • •

"Martin, Martin, do not die yet! Wait! I have something I must tell you." My eyes fluttered open, but objects swam in and out of the blackness. A skull on a shelf against the wall seemed to glow, then faded away. The large wooden cross over the simple altar kept getting larger, then smaller again. Anselm was sitting on the floor holding me up so that my back rested against his chest. His arms were around me, supporting my body. He held a folded cloth, torn from his habit, against my bleeding shoulder, trying to stanch the flow. I could see the amount of gore on my clothes and his, as well as a spreading puddle on the floor. The place where he held the cloth burned steadily and yet seemed to be in someone else's body. I moved my eyes around as well as I was able and saw Robert standing a little distance away, though he too faded in and out. Beyond him were two men with sheathed swords, all of them staring down at me.

I raised my hand to my neck. "Did he cut my throat?" I asked in a whisper.

"Just the skin of the throat." Anselm swallowed a sob. "You threw him off balance by turning so that he was unable to get the blade very far into your neck." His voice began to tremble and I could feel a shudder in his body, "But he did fearful damage to your shoulder," he drew a long tearful breath, "and I have not been able to get the blee, blee, bleeding to stop. The infirmarian is coming now, and we will pray that he can make you right." But I could feel him shaking his head.

"Anselm," I whispered, "what did you mean when you said 'Don't die yet?' Am I to die now?"

He stroked my hair, tenderly. He turned my face so that he could look into my eyes. Tears were running down his cheeks.

"Martin, what a marvelous thing you did!" He swallowed. "By disabling Godwin, you allowed me to get the advantage of him." He took both my hands and shook them gently. "We have stopped this terrible practice of kidnapping and abusing boys."

"Did he confess?" I asked.

"Oh yes." Anselm allowed his triumph to enter his voice.

"When Robert brought in the Sheriff's men, Godwin readily confessed.

"He knew he would be tortured if he did not tell everything. He has done his terrible work for almost twenty years, but his loyalty is to himself. He was only too glad to give up his employer and his associates." Anselm now sounded proud. "He told us of Benedict's role, which Robert's testimony will confirm. Godwin was the chief procurer and panderer for the Duke of Beaulisle. The Duke is the leader of a secret society of wealthy and powerful men devoted to that particular sin. Godwin provided for them all, sampling what he called 'the pleasures' even before he delivered the boys to their new masters."

While Anselm held me, Robert leaned over and held a leathern cup of water to my lips. I tried to drink, but couldn't swallow much. My body seemed to becoming numb. He said, "Martin, you have been a good friend to all of us. You really did what you said you would do. We novices will be safe now. God must bless you," he sobbed, "and also Brother Anselm."

I held up my hand. I forced words out, coughing between them. "Robert, you are the hero. Remember I told you that you would be a hero? Neither Anselm ... nor I ... could have ... could have ... overcome Preston without ..."

My voice was failing, but I croaked a whisper, "But there were others. Some men helped Preston. Two others I think, on this side of the river." I held up my hand. I forced words out, coughing between them.

Anselm spoke into my ear. "We have no way of knowing who they are. The Duke's men most likely. And it is certain we cannot get at the Duke without the King's support. And that will be difficult."

"Even...Godwin... confess...?" I managed to choke out.

"Even so. The Duke serves the King and the King owes him money. A great deal of money. It is probably more than we can risk to lay accusations against him. The Duke and his friends are perfectly willing to sacrifice Godwin. But I told you that the veterans of Crecy think they are inviolate. And mostly they are right."

I closed my eyes again. Every part of my body was in pain, but I felt as though I were moving out of this body. Everything seemed to be moving far away. If I could ever get to see Will again I would tell him to look into law-enforcement in the fourteenth century. "Oh, Will," I thought, "I don't want to die here and now. I want to hold you, to feel your hands on me, and your lips. I feel as though I could really surprise you with my love-making. Oh, God, please let me try."

I heard Robert's voice. "Is he gone?" I opened my eyes again and looked at him.

"Robert-Preston - did you kill?" I whispered.

"Ah, he still speaks." Robert murmured to Anselm. He took my hand and held it gently. "No, Martin, I only knocked him unconscious. But he stayed that way long enough for the Sheriff's men to take him, too."

I faded further but still had so many questions. "Did - only take boys - St. Martin's?"

Now Anselm spoke again. "No, they had many sources, widely spaced in place and time, so that connections would not be made. But Godwin had a special affection for St. Martin's. He said, without the least bit of shame, that his career began there. And I suspect that it began with me. He seemed rather proud and defiant even though he will die for his crimes."

I closed my eyes. I was passing into unconsciousness again and fought against it. Through the mists, I saw the parade of people on the road from Canterbury, then the see-through lady smiling at me. "Anselm, why...?" I murmured, but was unable to get the words together into a coherent sentence. "Cooper... bones... humming... gift..."

"Do you know, Brother, what he is trying to say?" Anselm nodded.

"Robert, you and the Sheriff's men wait outside. When the infirmarian arrives you can bring him in. And someone needs to get a priest to shrive this lad. But right now I must be alone with Martin."

"Martha," he said when we were alone. "I believe you can hear me still. There is much that I must tell you and very little time for either of us, for I am also going to die, this time truly and completely. So, if you can hear what I am saying, blink your eyelids several times." I did so.

"Good. Martin is dying. Martha is not. Martha cannot die in the fourteenth century because Martha is of the twentieth century. Martha is the reliving of Martin."

I blinked my eyelids furiously. I grabbed his hand and held it as tightly as I could. In my mind I said, "You mean reincarnation?"

I don't know this term, reincarnation. If it means you have lived before and will live again, then yes, that is what I mean. Most people do so. Perhaps all. It is very unusual for anyone to be as aware of all the experiences in the various periods in which they have lived as you are. But it is because you were so aware that you were uniquely able to help me. The first time you, as Martha, were in this place, this Chapel of Bones, it had a special meaning for you, because you died here, as Martin. Martin is the boy who was kidnapped and killed because I did not act to save him. You were the person I was seeking all these centuries, because you were Martin, living a new life in the person of Martha. I could atone my sin because you were the right person." He held me tightly. "Oh my dear girl, you have been a blessing."

I lifted his hand to my lips. "Anselm, have you known this all along?"

"I knew that I had to find the person who had lived before as Martin, yes, that I knew. It took a longer time to figure out how to do it.

"There are mysteries here that will never be explained to human satisfaction. Martin must die, because Martin died. But this time he dies bravely, no longer a victim, but a victor. So Martha will no longer be a victim."

I thought, "Anselm, will I remember all this?"

"If you choose."

"Anselm, there are mists and clouds. I think I am going now."

"Wait, Martha, wait." His two warm hands enclosed my limp cold ones. "I have more I must tell you. Once I take you back, I will no longer be able to tell you this. I will finally die in the plague."

The mists were becoming thicker and Anselm's voice even in my head began to fade away. I was no longer aware of pain or cold.

I heard individual words: St. Peter's, piscina, parchments. "I'll remember those," I thought. "They all begin with 'p.' I heard other words, or parts of words: Bert, Celts, Romans, temple... and then I heard, ever so faintly, the words in Latin that I assumed were the last rites. I heard no more.

25
The Search 1952

WILL WAITED UNTIL the Coopers were both busy with chores. He ran down the lane to the woods surrounding the Chapel. He went from window to window, peering into each, but saw nothing more than he had seen the first time. The ground outside was covered thickly with fallen leaves now cemented in place with rain and frost. He walked around the perimeter, scuffing up the leaves with his feet, looking for anything that might indicate that Martha had been there. In a rhododendron shrub, amongst the frozen and shriveled leaves, he saw what seemed to be a bit of a leather strap. He had to get down on his knees and grope through the close branches to get to the center, and there in the very middle of the shrub, dripping wet, was Martha's knapsack. It still had in it her Country Life Picture Book, now curling, pages stuck together from dampness, a bra and a pair of panties, a toothbrush, a hairbrush and about £5. A new terror that had not previously occurred to him presented itself. She had been kidnapped!

The Canterbury police were polite, scrupulously polite, but it was evident from the questions they asked that they thought it was just a lover's tiff. A fat sergeant, his uniform tunic gapping slightly between the buttons leaned over his desk, smoothing his huge mustache with the back of his right hand, and said softly, "I know you are very upset, sir, but it is too soon for us to conclude that she was kidnapped. In most situations of this kind the missing party shows up after a week or so."

"What about her knapsack? She wouldn't have just left it. That book is her most precious possession." Will tried to compel the policeman to act by the urgency of his pleas.

"Sorry, sir The knapsack doesn't prove anything. I can think of a dozen reasons why she left it there." The policeman held up a hand to count his reasons. He held up one finger. "For example, she might have placed it there to hide it and forgotten where she put it." He held up a second finger. "Maybe she wanted to climb a tree." Will stood there shaking his head and looking more and more as though he might cry. The officer held up a third finger and then seemed to change his mind. "But suppose we put out a bulletin, sir, just to be on the safe side?

"Now was there any reason anyone would want to take your wife, sir? Did she come from wealth?"

She didn't, of course.

That began several days of Will going round to all the places they had gone to together on their earlier visit. Will had given Cooper a large part of his limited money to pay for the poster. He decided to use the $1000 they had left of their wedding money for a reward, though when translated into pounds it sounded pretty skimpy: £360 reward for information regarding the whereabouts of Martha Elizabeth Davis Morton.

"Now, now, my boy, that is a fortune to the average person," Mr. Cooper assured him.

The weather cleared and Will went to sit at the little table in the Cathedral Close where they had had tea, and from which Martha had run away to the Chapel. The snack bar was shuttered for the winter, but he could sit there and stare at the magnificent old structure. A file of little girls in school uniforms: short pleated navy skirt, navy blazer with school crest on the pocket, striped tie, cloche hat, and knee socks, led by a woman in a larger, longer version of the same uniform, came chattering by. Will watched them pass out of sight at the entrance to the Cathedral and wondered what Martha had looked like at that age.

He envisioned her face in front of him: lovely, straight little nose, those brown eyes with long lashes, a mouth that turned up on one side, as though on the brink of a wry smile. As he focused on this image, it began to change, and he saw the face become smaller, rounder, surrounded by a tangle of wavy red hair on a pillow.

He watched as she became the center of a vignette: Martha, unmistakable, but a very little girl, in bed staring up, her mother sitting to one side with a book open in front of her. Standing at the foot of the bed was a woman in a lace mop cap and long skirt, and the woman was transparent! The apparition turned and looked directly at him. She mouthed words at him that Will somehow knew were "Believe her."

Will continued to stare at this picture, unable to move or even blink, until eventually it faded and he was looking again at the buttresses and windows of the Cathedral. "Wow!" he said to himself, "where did that come from?"

He decided to distract himself by making a thorough tour of the Cathedral. The image of Martha as a little girl with the transparent woman looking down at her kept returning to him. He got up and went into the Cathedral. Walking down the center of the stately pillar-lined nave, he paused to gaze up at the fan vaulting in the ceiling of the Angel Tower. It was like the fans of Japanese dancers. He expected any moment for them to snap shut to reveal beautiful female faces. He kept looking and looking, straight upwards until the entire Cathedral began to sway and he felt as though he were about to faint. Falling into a chair set next to the aisle, he put his head down until the dizziness faded.

A hand grasped his elbow and a voice with a soft, cultured, English accent asked, "Hello, are you not feeling well?"

Will turned and saw a young woman about his own age, wearing a green raincoat and beret. Short, curly blond hair emerged from the hat and very blue eyes in porcelain-white skin regarded him with concern.

Will smiled shakily at her. "Thank you. Breakfast was a long time ago I guess, but I'll live."

The woman nodded her head, releasing his arm. "If you need to get something to eat, there's a nice little tea shop in the undercroft," she said.

"Thanks, but I'll sit here and rest for a while, I think."

She nodded. "Yes, I was doing the same. Good place to collect one's thoughts, or not think at all."

Will sat there with his eyes closed, trying to breathe deeply and empty his mind. He heard the creaking of a chair as the woman next to him shifted in her seat. He became aware of her scent. It was lavender. He remembered giving a bottle of it to his mother for her birthday one year. It seemed terribly English. No young American woman would wear it, he thought. He opened his eyes and glanced over to find those blue eyes staring openly at him. The scent seemed to fit with the hair and the pale skin. "You look very sad," she said softly.

"Is it that obvious?" He gave her a wry smile and ducked his head. "And here I thought I was the strong silent suffer-in-silence type."

"Sometimes it helps to talk about it." The woman looked serious and sympathetic. Will looked at her, trying to decide whether he felt like talking about Marti to a strange woman. Someone else who could know what a failure as a husband he had been. He shook his head. "I don't want to bore you," he said.

"I know you Yanks are usually sticklers for proprieties, but would you let me buy you a cup of tea?"

"Never let it be said that Will Morton is a stickler." He grinned at her. "I'd like that."

"I'm Penelope Simmons." They shook hands. Up the steps and into the northwest transept they went. He followed her out the door into the cloister. "The stairs to the tea shop are out here. And it was through this very door that the four murderers of Saint Thomas entered." Will nodded. Why had they murdered him? He had heard the story once, but couldn't recall it now and anyhow who cared? He was staring at the slim ankle and the gently swaying hips of the woman in front of him. He smiled and then shook his head as for an instant her hair turned into a long red braid. "Yeah, yeah, I know," he told the image as it faded.

Sitting in front of a fire in the undercroft, with their tea cups in front of them, they smiled again at each other. "So," the young woman said, reaching out to hold Will's wrist, "Why are you so sad?"

Will looked down at her long fingers and then over at the fire in the fireplace. He could feel a quickening of his pulses. What the hell was he doing? He was a married man, even if his wife had left him. "Penelope, I'm married," he said. "I think I'm accepting your tea under false pretenses."

She laughed, her voice high pitched and bubbly. "Will, drinking tea is not *necessarily* a precursor to a love affair." She blushed, the rose color traveling up from her neck onto her cheeks. She laughed again. "Nor is it an act of infidelity. So what's the problem? Had a tiff?"

"Look, I'll probably never see you again… I mean, do you really want to know? It's a crazy story. My wife disappeared, or maybe she left me. Or maybe she was kidnapped, or maybe she lost her mind. I'm trying to find her and there's a man I know, who lives down on St. Martin's Lane, who is helping me." Will stopped for breath and saw Penelope staring at him warily. "Look, I'm sorry. Thanks for taking pity on me. But I need to get back to this guy's house. And thanks for the tea."

"Are you going back there now?" Penelope picked up her gloves and rose to her feet as Will did.

"Yeah, I'd better." Will held out his hand toward her, but she continued to look into his eyes.

"I live out just beyond St. Martin's Lane." She pulled on her gloves and took Will's arm. "Why don't we walk together and you can tell me about her, or we can talk about the weather."

With Penelope's gloved hand resting lightly on his arm, they walked out of the Cathedral Close. Will glanced into the window of the Boot's Chemists as they emerged onto St. George's Street. He was startled to see this stranger so close to him in the reflection. She was tall, almost his height. Definitely not the image he was used to seeing on his arm.

He looked directly at her and she smiled at him. He looked back at the shop window and noticed, this time, a pyramid of boxes of Enos Liver Salts, with a picture of a satisfied female user, grey hair piled up in a pompadour, her head wreathed with flowers. It was repeated over and over. As he gazed at them, the image changed, one by one, into the face of the transparent woman. He pulled up short in front of the window, almost tripping Penelope as he did so. He stared at the dozens of repeated images. Penelope glanced at where Will was staring and looked back at him.

"A fan of liver salts are you? Surely you are too young to need such a thing."

"Penelope, does anything strike you as odd about the picture on those packages?"

"No. Just the usual smiling user. Late middle-aged matron, I would guess. They've probably been using that picture since Victoria's day. What is it that you see, then?"

The illusion evaporated and Will murmured, "Nothing. I keep imagining I see things."

"Oh, you poor thing. Worried about your wife seeing you with a strange woman?" Penelope blushed again and tinkled her bell-like laugh. "Would she tear me limb from limb - or you perhaps?"

"Naw, she'd probably say, 'Oh good. Now maybe he'll leave me alone."

26
Return 1952

I MURMURED AND shifted in my bed and heard the crackling of fallen leaves, felt a hard lumpy surface, a dampness and then a chill underneath me, as though I were lying on something icy. The air smelled of earth and rotting vegetation. I opened my eyes and felt for whatever was poking me. I pulled out a rough piece of mortar about six inches long with a small piece of bone stuck into it. I closed my eyes tightly, shook my head hard and then opened them again. It was still sitting in my hand. It looked like those embedded in the walls of the Chapel of Bones. I laid it gently down next to me. I raised up on one arm and looked around. I was not in a bed but out of doors, in some woodsy place. Bare branches hung above me, undulating slowly in a slight wind. Somewhere in the distance a rook was cawing. The sky was heavily grey, as though it might snow at any moment. I was lying on a bed of brown leaves. I shook my head again, rubbed my eyes. Then I sat up very slowly.

Just beyond the trees in front of me, I could see the small stone building. A man in a monk's habit was walking toward it.

"Anselm, wait." I scrambled to my feet and started to run toward him. He stood in front of the door of the Chapel of Bones. He turned to look at me. It *was* Anselm, but he didn't seem to know me.

"Anselm, it's me. Martin. What am I doing out here in the cold? What happened? Didn't I die?"

I stopped. I felt all along my neck which seemed perfectly intact. My shoulder, however, had the remains of a wound, scabbed over and almost healed. I looked at my hand.

"There's not even any blood," I mumbled. "I'm alive. I'm ok." I shouted toward his retreating figure. I started to run after him again.

Halfway there I tripped over a half-hidden tree root and fell onto one knee. I wasn't hurt, but my blue jeans got quite muddied in the process. Blue jeans? I ran my hands over my heavy pea coat, looked down at my grimy sneakers. I put my hands to my head and felt the cabled pattern of a knitted cap. A long heavy braid came from beneath it. I pulled it over my shoulder and stared at it its thickness and coppery shine. I pushed my hand under the cap and felt the hair on the top of my head. I hadn't been aware of holding my breath, but I exhaled deeply.

But I had to catch Anselm. I hopped up and started toward the Chapel again, just in time to see the heavy door closing behind a sandaled foot.

"Anselm, why won't you wait?" I shouted. I ran up to the door and tried the latch but it was firmly, implacably locked. I banged on it. "Anselm! Open up." I shouted, but my words echoed, *open up, open up,* in the empty silent forest. I ran around, rubbing a spot of grime off the glass of each narrow pointed window and looking at the interior from each one. There was nothing inside. Nothing. It was as empty and forgotten-looking as that first day in October when we had come here with Mr. Cooper. Cooper or Anselm? Which one? I brushed away a sudden welling of tears.

So I was back. I blew a breath. Would I even recognize things in the twentieth century? I sank down onto the door step and wrapped my arms around my knees. Suddenly I felt as though my bones were water. I had just done something so remarkable, so beyond imagining.

Was I even the same person? I hugged myself and could feel the swell of my breasts. I was back in my woman's body, but something was different. I was stronger, I thought. Bolder. I'd stood up to them. I'd done something I could never have done before. Then my mind turned immediately to Will. I'd run away from him, and who knows how much time had passed since then. Now I wanted to see him. But would Will still want me?

I became aware of the distant sound of something familiar, something I had not heard in a long time. It was so familiar, so much a part of the background that I had not noticed it before. A rumbling sound, a straining high-pitched whine. A truck! An engine struggling up the hill on the High Road, then a whoosh of air brakes and shifting of gears when the truck reached the top of the hill at the entrance to St. Martin's Lane.

I moved over to the stump of a long-gone tree, stared at the chapel and tried to figure out what to do now. All the time I had been away I'd thought about coming back. I'd wanted to experience the middle ages first hand and to help Anselm defeat that evil, and at the same time I'd wanted to be in the twentieth century again. Suddenly, I was almost overwhelmed by my desire to see Will. I wanted to share with him what I had seen, what I had found out. I thought about him now, how he had looked when I left him. So hurt, so angry. I imagined taking his face in my hands and kissing his forehead.

The last time I had been in this place I had gone inside the Chapel with Anselm and agreed to go back with him to his time. I was trying to remember something else I did, just before that. There was a huge rhododendron bush next to the entrance to the Chapel. My backpack. It had a change of clothes, I remembered, a little money and my book. I had stuffed it into the middle of the bush's tangle of leaves and branches before I went into the chapel with Anselm that day.

The wind suddenly began blowing harder and I shivered. I was aware of how cold I was and how hungry. I couldn't just sit here. I reached inside the bush, pulling the branches apart and feeling around. No one ever came here, Mr. Cooper had told us. So I could expect that somewhere in the middle of this bush would be my backpack. I could take the money and get something to eat and a ticket for the first train back to London, and to Will.

Some snowflakes began to swirl around as I grappled into the middle of the branches. My hand encountered nothing. I approached it from another side. Again nothing. Beginning to feel panicky, I walked all around the bush, scuffing up the fallen leaves as I peered into it and onto the ground around it. My eye caught a tiny square of red cardboard partly emerging from under a matted pile of leaves. I picked it up and looked carefully. It was sodden and faded but I could just make out the letters "NAL" and the word "carry". It was part of the label that had been attached to my backpack when we came on to the Netherlands America Line's S.S. Ryndam. It had distinguished the carry-on luggage from the stuff that was to be placed in the hold for the passage. Well, my backpack had been here, but obviously wasn't any longer.

It was getting dark and I needed to get moving. I would freeze to death if I stayed here. I could barely make out the path back through the bushes onto St. Martin's Lane. I would go out onto the High Road and hitch a ride. As I trudged along, I could see the windows of the houses, brightly lit and looking so cozy. In the house where someone had peered out of closed curtains the last time I was here, I could see a woman curled in a large green upholstered chair, reading a newspaper, a ginger cat on the chair arm. She never looked up as I passed by. I walked past Mr. Cooper's house. Would he remember me? Maybe he would lend me the train fare to London, or let me just get warm by his fire? What could I tell him? Nothing. My story was too weird and I was too weary to dream up a plausible reason for being here. I could hear the trucks and cars passing at the end of the lane, flying by in both directions, the vehicles coming from Canterbury speeding up once they got to the top of the hill, those from London zooming down in the other direction. I couldn't decide which way I needed to go, nor where to stand to get someone to stop for me. I stood there in a paralysis of indecision. I walked a few feet along the main road, stopped, walked back. I brushed away the tears running down my face. My teeth were chattering. My stomach was growlingly empty. I was unbelievably, desperately tired. One foot shambled after the other. I couldn't walk another step. I lowered myself onto an embankment rising from the shoulder of the road and just sat there, unable to move, my eyes falling closed.

In a quiet lull between the coming and going vehicles, I heard footsteps of people walking up the hill, one a heavy hiking-boot sound, the other the tap-tap of a woman's high heels. I scooted up the embankment and made myself small, hoping they would not look up. They'd think I was crazy to be sitting by the side of the road as the snow fell.

"No, I've never actually laid eyes on the Chapel of Bones, though I heard rumors when I was at school that there was such a place. One doesn't just wander down St. Martin's Lane. The people there are very protective of their privacy." It was a woman's voice, high-pitched and rather tinkly. A man's voice, lower, with indistinguishable words, said something in reply. Then the woman said, "Is that true? And you actually saw bones in the mortar? How thrilling!"

An oncoming headlight illuminated the couple as they came over the rise. A tall young blonde wearing a green raincoat and a beret was holding the arm of a very tall young man. My heart started beating fast, clouds came before my eyes and I felt as though I were dying all over again. I started to call out "Will," then clamped a hand over my mouth. He'd found someone else. It served me right. I sat very still, wanting to jump up and say, "Take your hand off my husband." I had left the little knife sticking in Abbot Godwin, or I might have been tempted to attack her. And she was as tall as he was. He was mine, God damn it! But maybe he didn't think so. "Will," the words screamed in my head, "I love you. I want you. Don't go." But the only sound I made were the snuffles as I tried to keep my nose from running. I remained immobile while they walked by.

As they reached the opening of St. Martin's Lane, they stopped and faced one another, the woman dropping hold of Will's arm.

"It's been nice walking with you, Penelope. Thanks for the tea and the sympathetic ear." Will held out his hand and the woman grasped it. She lifted her face to him and kissed him gently on his cheek. He started to put his arms around her and then abruptly allowed them to fall to his sides.

"Good luck, Will. I hope you find your wife. She's a lucky woman." They shook hands and the woman walked on as Will turned into the lane. *I hope you find your wife. He'd been telling her about me.*

I hopped up and followed him, trying to get enough saliva into my desert-dry mouth to call out to him. The door to Mr. Cooper's house opened and he walked out, a little dog on a leash just behind him.

"What luck, Will?" Mr. Cooper called out, "find anything interesting?" Will shrugged. "Not really sir. At least not what I was looking for. Here, I'll take Chaucer out to the road, no sense in both of us freezing." He came down almost to where I was standing, but didn't see me as he watched the dog intently.

"Hi, Sugar," I said softly.

Will jumped and stared at me. "Marti?" he whispered. He reached out and touched my cheek. He moved closer and stroked my head, lifted my braid, touched one shoulder, then the other. I raised up on tip-toe took his face into my hands, brought it down to my level and kissed his forehead. He raised his head and looked at me with complete wonder. "Oh my God! Marti. You've come back." He reached out and took me into his arms, leaning over to press his lips onto mine for a long, long kiss, as though he were drinking me in and never wanted to stop. When we finally came up for air, he opened his jacket and pulled me inside. I lay my face on his warm chest. Finally, I looked up to him and smiled through the tears that were streaming down my face. "If you like, I could cut my hair and dye it blond." I said. "But I'll never be anything but short."

27
Don't Let Me Go 1952

WILL JUST HELD me in his arms. With Chaucer yapping and jumping around us, I slipped my arms around Will's back and rested my face against his chest.

Will repeatedly kissed the top of my head as he held me. I breathed in his clean clothes and under them his healthy, clean skin.

"Don't ever let me go," I said. I hoped I had not brought back the unwashed smell of my body in the 14th century. The way Will was nuzzling the top of my head made me feel that I was my old self. Now I knew how I would approach the whole subject of my absence. His body spoke to me, but Will said nothing. We would have remained there, I think, until we turned to stone, or we both fell down from exhaustion, but a clearing of a throat and the words, "Ahem, may I take it that this is the famous Martha?" brought us back to where we were, and to Mr. Cooper's presence. We looked at him and I reached out one hand and said, "It is nice to see you again, Mr. Cooper."

"Ah, yes, but you see... oh, never mind. We'll explain it all later. We are so glad to see you. Will, let's get this young woman indoors, it's getting quite chilly."

There followed a nourishing tea, with welsh rarebit, stewed apples, meringues, toast and marmalade, cucumber sandwiches, chocolate cake, and a parade of other goodies that I couldn't stop eating, to Mrs.

Cooper's gratification. "Oh, how lovely to be so young and slim that you can eat with such abandon!" I was treated to a detailed relating of Will's and Mr. Cooper's efforts to find me, complete with Mr. Cooper's complaints about the chap who had been impersonating him and how they had tried to sort out which people he had spoken to. "I really need to get to the bottom of this. It is outrageous to have someone going around pretending to be me!" All during this recounting, Will couldn't keep his hands off me, resting his hand on my shoulder, or holding the hand that was not propelling food into my mouth. Chaucer also refused to be parted from me, lying at my feet with his nose on my instep throughout the meal. Everyone politely chattered, and I realized they were waiting for me to begin my story. But all I could say was, "Oh, how delicious!" or "I'd forgotten how good this tasted."

An oil painting of a young man in an eighteenth century military uniform set in a heavily carved gold frame hung over the sideboard. The young man was clean-shaven and looked out of the portrait with a slightly amused expression. He looked even more like Anselm than Mr. Cooper did. I turned to Mr. Cooper and asked, "Is that an ancestor? He looks familiar."

"Great, great grandfather. The wife chose that one from the whole stable of family pictures, didn't you, my dear?"

"Well, I was a bit torn, this one was a real reprobate it was said, but I liked the way the red coat went with the carpeting."

I smiled to myself. *Were you keeping things from me, Anselm?* I thought. A yawn popped out of me before I could get my hand over my mouth.

I put down my fork and smiled at them all, feeling almost drunk with good feelings. Then my eyes kept drooping, and I shook my head to jolt them open again.

Finally Mr. Cooper said, "Will, you'd better put this tired young woman to bed, so that in the morning she can give us a full accounting of her whereabouts during the past two weeks." My eyes opened completely and I looked at him. I opened my mouth but no words came out.

It was bad enough to contemplate trying to tell Will, but what could I say to these kind strangers?

By the time Will supported me down the hallway from the overheated sitting room to the mid-winter chill of the unheated guest room, I was struggling to keep awake, stumbling between the impossibly tall pieces of furniture that lined the way from the front to back of the house. Will put me to bed, stripping the clothes from my pliant body, as my bones melted into the mattress. He pulled the tent-like flannel nightgown lent me by Mrs. Cooper over my head.

As I snuggled under the feather comforter, descending into an ever-deepening sleep, I saw Anselm turn and wave to me from the door of the Chapel of Bones. Then Robert offered his dagger to me. I saw the abbot smirking at his bound hands. I saluted them all, now victor, no longer victim. Then another parade of pictures: Mrs. Freedom kneading dough and looking at me with pride, my father staring into my eyes then looking away, burying his head in his hands. Each image grew fainter, farther and farther away.

28
The Short Version 1952

I WAS AWAKENED by a passing car light moving over my face then down the wall next to the bed. Will lay on his side, having thrown back the covers from his waist up. I could see his naked chest and sleeping face in the light of a street lamp. It seemed almost to glow. I had never seen anything more beautiful. I moved my finger over him, gossamer light, stroking his face from temple to jaw and back again, then around his ear and along his hairline across the back of his neck. He turned over and opened his eyes very wide. They glittered in the grey light, and I could see the sparkling of his tears welling up. I kept touching him ever so gently, as though he were some fragile precious object; his neck, circling his Adam's apple, outlining each collarbone with the tiniest strokes; the strong bones of his shoulder, the relaxed muscles that enfolded it. I moved my fingers down his arm, smoothing the hair, as he followed my hand with his eyes. I located the bones of his elbow, traced the veins into his hand, then straightening and bending each finger, lifting his hand to my lips to kiss each knuckle. I felt almost in a trance, my actions being directed by something not in my head, although I was acutely aware of the electric current that flowed from each stroke my finger made.

He swiveled his hand around so that now my hand was enfolded in his, and he kissed my wrist. He then he took my other hand so that both of mine were wholly contained within his so much larger ones.

"Do you know how much I love you," he whispered, "how empty my life has been without you?" He stroked my cheek. "First I was so mad at you. Then I was drowning in hurt and self-pity."

"Will, I'm so sorry to have put you through all that."

"And then I just wanted you back."

"Oh, Will," I whispered back. "I love you so much. I've worried that I might not get back to you. That you might not want me any more."

Will sat up now, and reached over to turn on the bedside lamp. We sat up in bed, tailor-fashion, facing each other with knees touching. He reached up inside the wide flannel sleeves to hold my upper arms. Tears were trickling down his cheeks. "I kept thinking, kept regretting, while you were gone, that I had never told you what a marvelous, brilliant, beautiful, sexy woman you are."

I couldn't answer, but tears began to run down my cheeks, too.

"I want to keep telling you, showing you how much I, I..." He gave a sob, then pulled me toward him so that he could kiss me.

"No, Will." I detached his hands and pushed him back onto the pillow. "Let me show you first. Don't move."

I leaned over his chest, and continued my examination and my gentle stroking. I took his nipples between my thumbs and forefingers and kissed first one and then the other, back and forth like a metronome, the music approaching crescendo.

"Wow!" he said. "Oh-my-God!" I uncovered him further, kissing and stroking him down the length of his abdomen, not hesitating at all when I reached his groin. Joy poured out of the smile that radiated from my face. "God, you're a beautiful man," I whispered and pulled myself up to reach his mouth with my lips.

He seemed to be holding his breath. His body felt as though he were willing himself to be totally still to keep from exploding, from erupting into a fireworks display of dancing bones and sinews. I moved myself up onto him and rode him to climax.

"My turn," he said with a delighted chuckle. He rolled himself over onto me and took over.

When we were finally spent and exquisitely exhausted, facing each other side by side, Will looked over at me and, on a whoosh of exhalation, said, "Oh Jesus!" He kissed my eyelids, my cheeks and then my mouth, as gently and tenderly as I had done his. He put his hands on either side of my face and looked into my eyes. "You are amazing!" he said.

We lay silently on our backs, holding hands, each of us in our own reverie. Will raised up and looked at me again.

"Marti, I don't want you to talk about it until you are ready. And I promise to believe whatever you tell me. But you know that we can't have a real life until you are willing to share these secrets you've been keeping from me."

I nodded my head. "I know that, Will. And Sugar, I did find what I went away to find. I'm fine now. I really am."

He took my hand, then looked straight into my eyes. "OK, for openers, let me tell you something." He described the image he had, while sitting in the Cathedral Close, of me as a little girl and the transparent woman who looked at him and said, "Believe her."

My mouth fell open. "Will, what you saw. It really happened. When I was very little I started seeing her. I called her 'The see-through lady' and she came to me a number of times when I was in trouble. She saved my life!"

"But not from being raped?"

I thought about that for a moment, feeling quite calm and rather detached. "No," I said, "I've never understood why she didn't help me then. I thought maybe she was only there when I was a little kid. But I was still pretty young when he did that to me."

"Who?" he said, "Who did that to you? If I find him, I think I might kill him.

I looked back at my husband. He again seemed to be holding his breath. I shook my head, feeling sad, but no longer particularly angry. "Will," I said, "what sort of pathetic specimen of a father forces himself on his twelve-year old-daughter?"

"Oh, Jesus," he said, "That foul son of a bitch." He reached over to stroke my cheek. "God, Marti, what you've been through!" I moved my head sideways and down so that my cheek rested on his hand. I moved into his arms.

"But I am a different person now, Will. My parents can't stand in my way, in our way, ever again!" I pushed myself away and looked up at him. But now what am I going to tell the Coopers?"

Will pointed vigorously at his chest. "How about me? Don't you think you need to tell me all sorts of things, first?"

"OK, I'll give you the short version, right now, and the rest later. But you need to remember what the lady said!"

"Right, I will! I promise."

"OK, remember when we were here in the fall and I told you I was taken by a monk into the 14th century, where I was a boy, and all that?"

Will looked warily at me. "I remember," he said, but he seemed to be pulling back from me as though to withdraw from what was coming. I could see him physically forcing himself to lean forward again and take my hand.

I held his hands even more firmly. "Will, you promised!"

Will inhaled deeply. "I know. I believe you. I really do believe you," he said. "Tell me."

"Well, the other Mr. Cooper was a monk named Anselm, and he took me back to the 14th century to the monastery of St. Martin's. He had been walking the earth looking for me for the past six hundred years because he knew that I could help him undo a sin that he had committed. He would then be able to go to his eternal rest. For the last two weeks—it sure seemed longer than that—-I've been a boy novice, and wait until I tell you all about what the 14th century was like! And by allowing myself to be captured by a terrible ex-abbot who stole boys to make prostitutes out of them, I was able to help Anselm capture him. I stabbed him with a dagger, but he stabbed me, too. The boy that I was then died, but Anselm had rescued the real me and captured the abbot, so Anselm undid his sin and and I was able to come back to you." I stopped to catch my breath. "Will, I feel now that because I was able to stand up to someone who abused children and help defeat him, I'm no longer that little girl victim. I'm whole again.

"But before I died, oh dear God, wait 'til you hear this, Anselm told me where to look for the parchments that are St. Augustine's original journal!

"And that's the short version of the story!"

I looked at Will's face and my lips started to quiver. "Will, you don't believe me!"

Will held his head in his hands. He bit his lips. He didn't say anything for what seemed like a long time. He just looked up and stared thoughtfully at my face. Finally he shook his head. He grinned at me. "Yes, I do, Marti, I really do. And you know what? I can't wait to hear the long version," he said, and he took my hand and kissed my palm.

We both dozed dreamily, holding hands. Each of us would reach over, every so often, to stroke or touch the other until we both fell back to sleep.

We were awakened by the sound of Mrs. Cooper humming as she ran water into a kettle and the scent of bread toasting. The sky outside the window was still black, but some birds were chirping half-heartedly, so it was definitely becoming day.

"Good morning, lovely wife." Will reached over and kissed me. "Where are we going to look for that journal?"

"Ha! That got your interest, didn't it?" I sat up, pulled the cover up to my chest, and squinted into the distance.

"Hm. I'm not sure...wait a minute. I said the words all begin with p. St. Peter's, piscina, parchment. I remember hearing that just as I was passing away. I think that means we have to look behind the piscina in St. Peter's church for a parchment. How do you suppose we do that?"

Suddenly Will threw back the cover, jumped up, and ran over to the chair where his clothes were carefully folded. I gave a happy little chuckle, as I looked at his long naked shape. He reached into his jacket pocket and took out a folded piece of paper. "This came after you disappeared," he said. "I read it because I thought it might give a clue as to where you'd gone."

I opened the sheet of heavy linen paper. It had the crest of Canterbury Cathedral at the top. My shaking hand caused the paper to give a little whispery sound.

"It's from the chief archivist of the library at Canterbury Cathedral," I told Will in a hushed voice.

"Dear Mrs. Morton." I read aloud, "I have made arrangements for you to look at the medieval documents ..." I looked up at Will with astonishment. "I never thought they would even answer me, much less let me in. Will, they're going to let me see the records of the additions and renovations to St. Peter's church in the mid 14th century"

"Why do you need to see the additions and stuff from the 14th Century?"

"Well, at first I was just curious about what parts survived from the original Roman building and I had read that major renovations had taken place in the 14th Century. But now that I've been told where St. Augustine's journal is hidden in the structure, maybe I can figure out how to get to it."

I continued to read aloud. "These documents: plans and drawings of the church, before and after the renovations, dum, dum, dum... marked dum, dum... chronicler of St. Martin's Abbey, ... as you speculated in your request, indicate which parts of the church antedate the changes made in that period.

"I was right!" I said triumphantly.

"If you will call at my office at 10:30 in the morning on 7th Feb., 1953, I will arrange for you to study them in the company of one of our staff members."

"Marti, that's fantastic!" Will said. "I'd really love to come with you."

"Oh, Will!" I reached over and kissed him. "Would you? I do want you to share all of this with me. How is your Latin for reading early medieval script?"

I started to put on my bra. "Now help me figure out," I said, "what to tell the Coopers."

About the Author

Joan Oltman has a master's degree in creative writing and two additional master's degrees in education. Her stories, poems, and articles have been published in literary and women's magazines, and she serves as editor for several newsletters and a local magazine.

Oltman has always loved the medieval period and has visited monasteries, cathedrals, castles, museums, and other significant historical sites to learn their secrets.

Oltman worked as a social worker and spent twenty years teaching elementary school. She has also taught in various graduate education programs.

Oltman is a recent widow. She has three children, six grandchildren, many nieces and nephews, and two great-nephews

Made in the USA
Middletown, DE
03 February 2017